MAGICAL MISCHIEF
MAGIC & METAPHYSICS ACADEMY
BOOK 1

LAURA GREENWOOD
LAINIE ANDERSON

© 2019 Laura Greenwood & Lainie Anderson

All rights reserved. This book or parts thereof may not be reproduced in any form, stored in any retrieval system, or transmitted in any form by any means – electronic, mechanical, photocopy, recording or otherwise – without prior written permission of the published, except as provided by United States of America copyright law. For permission requests, write to the publisher at "Attention: Permissions Coordinator," at the email address; lauragreenwood@authorlauragreenwood.co.uk.

Visit Laura Greenwood's website at:

www.authorlauragreenwood.co.uk

Visit Lainie Anderson's website at:

www.laboruff.com

Cover Design by Ammonia Book Covers

Magical Mischief is a work of fiction. Names, characters, places, and incidents are the products of the author's imagination or are used fictitiously. Any resemblance to actual persons, living or dead, businesses, companies, events, or locales is entirely coincidental.

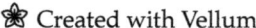 Created with Vellum

The first day at a new academy is never easy, especially not for Lou.

Home-schooled until she was eighteen, she's now facing academy for the first time with no idea what to expect. With eccentric dorm mates, frenemies coming out of her ears, and the most popular guys in school showing interest in her, Lou starts to feel like she's in over her head.

Does she have what it takes to survive her time at the academy?

-

Magical Mischief is book one of the Magic and Metaphysics Academy trilogy. It is filled with frenemies, a really evil book, and a reverse harem romance.

CHAPTER 1

Passing through the magical barrier went without an issue, which was surprising. I thought that there'd be a crackle or a bang or *something*. I hoped the rest of my time at the academy wouldn't be as blah. Surely the teachers would have lots to teach me.

Dad pulled the car to a stop right outside the front door. It was so close to the drive that I'd only have to walk a few feet. "Have you got everything you need?"

I rolled my eyes. "You know I do."

"This is hard for us, your mom and I..." He was pitiful, sitting in the driver's seat, watching his baby go off to college. Not pitiful enough for me to stay, however.

"Had a hard time letting me come here, I know."

But it was better than going into my adult life having been homeschooled. Mom and Dad just didn't have time to keep up with my learning anymore, which is how I'd managed to convince them to let me come to Magic and Metaphysics Academy once I'd turned eighteen. I had high hopes for the next three years.

"Your mom says good luck." He beamed at me in his absent-minded way.

"I know." She'd told me that before she went to bed this morning. I did find the fact she worked the night shift at the zoo amusing. It meant she ended up being stereotypically vampire and sleeping during the day.

"Tallulah..."

"Lou, please, Dad." I really didn't want anyone at the academy to overhear him calling me by my full name. This was my chance to actually make friends, not scare them off with *Tallulah*.

He shook his head. "Tallulah," he repeated. "We're really proud of you. Please don't forget to keep up with your schoolwork."

Man alive. Why couldn't he just let me out of the car? I didn't want this awkward talk. No one my age did. Dump and run was the preferred way for parents to drop their teenagers off at school, wasn't it?

"I will, Dad. But I have to go, or else I'll be late for

orientation." I was already nervous enough about starting a term later than everyone else, but there'd been no avoiding it. My parents had been on an expedition to find a species of magical monkey that everyone thought was extinct. It had been fascinating, even more so because they'd actually found information that would help people track the creature down.

"Alright. Your clothes should already be in your room; we sent them ahead."

I smiled fondly at him rather than pointing out that I already knew that. They'd involved me in all their planning, they always did. It was something I appreciated about them. They didn't treat me like I was an incompetent burden, even if they were a bit overprotective sometimes.

"Thanks, Dad." Leaning over, I kissed his cheek, knowing the gesture would go a good way to making him feel less frustrated with me.

"You're welcome, Lou. Call us on Friday."

My smile turned into a full beam when he used my preferred nickname.

"I will," I promised, finally seeing my escape on the horizon. I grabbed my bag and unclicked the door handle. "Love you."

"We love you, too." He waved frantically as I exited his car. "Make us proud."

"I'll try."

I swung my backpack over my shoulder and gave him a half-wave before turning around to face the enormous gothic building in front of me. Some people might find it imposing, but not me. I thought it was beautiful. There was a real elegance in the way the stone had been carved so delicately, and yet...wasn't something you'd want to get impaled on.

Huh, slightly macabre thought there. I should try and keep those in check when I'm around other people or they'll think I'm crazy. Of course, my experience had been people thought that anyway when they found out my parents were a vampire and a witch and that I was a hybrid. My kind was rare. Normally children took after one parent or the other, not both like me. Which also made me powerful. It was one of the reasons my parents had kept me home. They'd been scared of losing me, or me being injured, or any number of scary things that ultimately made them homeschool me.

With a sigh, I stepped forward, making my way through the huge front doors and into the academy. A small part of me would have preferred it if one of my parents was still with me, but the other part realized that was the quickest way to ensure that I ended up without any friends here. No one wanted to be that person.

Especially not at eighteen. The humans would have considered me an adult, but paranormal education continued on to twenty-one, at a minimum.

The halls were surprisingly quiet, almost as if the place was deserted. I checked my watch. Ten past nine. I supposed that would probably mean that the students were all in class. Maybe that was why no one was around. At least I was on time for my meeting with the headmaster.

I followed the instructions I'd been sent on the email, traveling through the academy and trying not to let the fired sconces intimidate me as their shadows danced against the stone walls. I'd heard that this place kept things traditional, but I hadn't realized it was quite this severe. At least they used email and the internet.

Turning into a corridor to the left, I breathed a sigh of relief to see the word headmaster scrawled across the door at the very end. I quickened my pace, hoping he'd see me sooner and not later. My appointment was technically at nine-thirty, and I didn't look forward to sitting around for twenty minutes waiting for him. That was a quick way to fry my nerves.

I knocked on the door as soon as I reached it. Part of me wanted to run away from the whole situation, but that wouldn't get me the education I needed.

"Come in," a woman's voice called.

I frowned. And here was me thinking that Headmaster Ian Schmidt was a man. Even so, I pushed the door open and found myself in a small reception room.

Ah. That made sense.

"Hi, I'm Ta—uh, Lou Davidson..." I trailed off. I should have practiced this more.

The woman smiled at me. "Take a seat, Miss Davidson, the headmaster will be ready for you in a moment." She pressed a button on her desk as she said it and my heart beat faster. Hopefully, that would just alert the man that I was there, and not call in a security detail to escort me from the premises. That would be just my luck.

The other door in the room swung open, and a portly man in his forties beckoned me in.

"Sit down, Miss Davidson, let me grab your file." He took it off the pile on his desk and sat down in his chair, gesturing for me to do the same.

"Thanks," I muttered, trying not to let the nerves show. I didn't know if it would do anything bad if he knew I was feeling anxious, but a big part of me just didn't want him to know.

"I've been following your parents' research papers for years," he told me. "They're fascinating people."

"Yes." I didn't engage him further. I'd spent my whole life with people talking to me about how much they loved my parents and what they did. It got kind of boring after a while.

"Are you looking to specialize in Zoomagology too?"

"No."

"What are you more interested in?"

"Plants," I admitted quietly. "I'm good with them."

"Magical botany then?"

I nodded. It wasn't something I'd ever told my parents about, scared they'd be unhappy with me spending more time with plants than with animals. But it was also something I was certain of. I'd always had a little bit of a green thumb, and I wanted to make the most of it.

"Ah, good. We have an after school club, the Greenies, you'll want to join. They have a prize show coming up towards the end of the year, and they'd do well to have someone with your knowledge on the team."

"My knowledge?" I squeaked. What did he know? Was he some kind of clairvoyant?

"From your entrance exam." He tapped the file he was holding.

"Oh." That made sense. I'd almost forgotten about that. It had been a fairly easy exam for me. I might have been taught from home, but my parents had done a good job of making sure my education had been thorough.

He handed me a bunch of papers and tapped the top of it. "There's information about all the extra-curricular activities in there. None of them are compulsory, but we do encourage our students to take part in at least one."

"Okay." I nodded, already feeling a little overwhelmed. Maybe this wasn't a good idea at all.

"There's also your class schedule and a map of the academy. Your dorm is clearly marked. You'll be sharing with two of our best students, Estelle Ford and Tyler Michaels. My secretary should have just gone to get them so they can show you around."

"Thank you." Meeting people already? This was officially the worst day ever. I'd hoped to have gotten my bearings before having to make small talk with other students.

"Attendance matters here. As does following the rules. You'll find those in there too. One of the most important is no drinking on campus. We know that students are going to want to, but we don't condone it here at all."

"Alright." I wasn't a big drinker anyway and suspected I would end up a lightweight if I even tried.

"Boys aren't allowed in the girls' dormitory and

vice versa. There are spells in place to stop that kind of sneaking around."

I gulped and nodded. Was that the kind of thing I'd have to deal with now?

"Excellent. I think that covers everything I have to say. If you go through the doors there, you should find your new dorm mates waiting. They'll show you where to go. The three of you are expected in class at ten."

"Thank you." I rose to my feet and scraped my chair back, eager to get out of there but not so that I could spend time with people I didn't know. I just wanted to be away from the headmaster.

He didn't say a word as I exited the room and found myself back in the reception room.

"Ah, Miss Davidson. May I introduce Estelle Ford and Tyler Michaels, they'll be showing you around the academy." The secretary gestured to two seated students.

They rose to their feet.

"I'm Estelle, this is Tyler," the first one said. She looked the furthest thing from an Estelle I could imagine. She was small and dainty, with a punky look completed by pink and black striped hair and a nose ring. Nope, nothing like I'd have expected an Estelle to look like.

"Hey." Tyler's voice was deep, husky. Dirty blonde

hair fell in front of her face. Well, I assumed she was a she. After all, we were sharing a dorm and that must mean she was female. Probably. If she said she was a she, then she would be. I nearly snickered at the silly rhyme in my head.

"Your stuff is already in the room," Estelle said. "We piled it on your bed."

"Thanks, yes. My parents sent it ahead," I responded needlessly.

"Come on, we'll show you where it is." Tyler turned and walked out the door, followed by Estelle. They waited for me in the hall, whispering to each other.

I paused for a moment, though I wasn't sure what I was waiting for. Maybe for the secretary to actually say something.

When she didn't, I trudged out of the room behind the two other students, already questioning what I'd done in deciding to come here. This could either be the best or the worst decision of my life. I hoped it was the former, but feared it might be the latter.

Only time would tell.

They took the long route, showing me classrooms and bathrooms, and all the dorm floors. The school was enormous, with four floors just for dorm rooms.

"There are eight or nine dorms on each floor with three to four people in each room."

"So, like a hundred and forty students here?" I asked incredulously. I hadn't expected there to be that many of us supernatural kids the same age at the same time.

"Well, yeah, but this isn't just shifters, like us." Tyler peered at me thoughtfully. "I can't get a vibe off you, by the way."

Shrugging, I didn't answer. "Does it matter?"

Estelle stopped dead on the stairs we were climbing. "Oh, yes. It does."

She continued on her way without explaining any further.

"Come on," Tyler said kindly, patting my hand on the banister. "We'll explain."

CHAPTER 2

"You alright?" Estelle asked.

"Huh? Yeah, fine. Just trying to get used to it all." I looked around the dorm room, trying to make sense of what I was seeing. The last thing I'd expected was three gigantic four-poster beds and a fire crackling in the grate along one wall, a huge window along the other.

"Oh, I get you. I thought this place was going to be a shit-hole when I first came. I was right in some ways, but the dorm rooms are pretty lush." She kicked off her shoes and collapsed onto the bed I presumed was hers. Tyler sat beside her, pulling a cell phone out of her pocket. The sounds of a game app filled the air.

"I guess I was expecting a row of uncomfortable single beds," I said.

"We're not in prison," Estelle pointed out.

"I know. I've just never been at an academy before..." Each bed had a giant cabinet on one side and a desk on the other.

"You were home-schooled?" She sat up so quickly, I could have sworn it gave me a bit of a headache.

Blinking, I nodded. "Yes. My parents are..."

Tyler's eyes widened. "Wait, Davidson? As in Barbara and Jerry Davidson?"

I rolled my eyes. "Yes, those are my parents."

"Cool." Estelle nodded as if it was the best thing I could have said. I didn't understand that, personally. But I'd go with it. To me, they were just Mom and Dad.

"So, as we were saying." Tyler sat up and twirled her fingers, producing a pen and paper. "You've got to keep this straight."

She set the pen on the paper where it wrote by itself, a simple spell. "The top of the hierarchy are the witches and vampires. They float through the other cliques, so be careful. They're always most loyal to each other."

Okay, I was both a vampire and witch, but I wasn't particularly cliquey. I would be happy being friends with Estelle and Tyler.

"Then you've got your shifters, they're the most common, and generally aren't terribly popular. Occasionally, one will rise through the ranks, but don't hold your breath if you're a shifter." Estelle nodded as Tyler spoke, watching the pen scrawl.

"You've got your Elms, they have elemental magic. They're always super mysterious and think they're better than everyone else, but in reality, nobody ever remembers they're there. Renee runs their group. She's okay, actually, but the rest of them are ridiculously anti-social. Some of them clique-hop into the Greenies, which brings us to the social-suicide club. The Greenies love doing nature magic."

I blanched. I loved nature magic. It made me feel the most alive.

"They always smell faintly of dirt, and if you ever touch them, you feel like you've been playing in potting soil." Tyler shuddered. "I can't stand being dirty."

And I loved it. My favorite thing was to be outside barefoot. It drove my parents crazy. Any time I was supposed to be working with an animal with them, I ended up wandering off and checking out the local foliage.

"Moving on," Tyler pointed at the pen and it wrote another name. "The Beckys."

Estelle rolled her eyes. "They're basic witches. Tend to hang around the Pires a lot, do their cheerleading when we have intramural games, which is like every weekend."

Tyler nodded. "Generally, they're harmless. Tomorrow's housewife. Andee runs that crew right now. Careful though, they can get pretty catty. You'll occasionally find a shifter in their ranks."

They acted like this was the most important information in the world. Surely what I'd learn at school was more important than who I hung around with?

"Is all this stuff really this important?" I asked, staring at the paper with wide eyes.

"Oh, yes," Estelle said. "If you cross the wrong people, you'll be miserable for the next three years."

That was potentially true. I'd have to be around these people twenty-four hours a day for three years until I was released as a licensed witch at twenty-one. I could go back to home-schooling, but I really wanted to do this like everyone else.

"Okay, I think I have it straight so far," I said skeptically.

"I feel like we're forgetting someone," Tyler said thoughtfully as she looked at the paper. "Oh, the Alts and the Chefs. They intermingle a lot. The Chefs are obsessed with potions and the Alts are like hipsters. Obsessed with learning archaic spells that nobody uses anymore. They say they're in pursuit of lost knowledge, but really they just like to read old books and wear black."

"They're not so bad," Estelle said. "I've spent some time with them. They hang out in the kitchens and make amazing coffee. Jean is their unofficial leader. She makes the best cappuccino ever." Estelle's eyes went all dreamy.

"Estelle is hard-core addicted to coffee," Tyler stage-whispered.

"Mmmm." She smiled. "I never want to stop."

"Shouldn't we get going to class?" I asked, looking at my watch and noticing it was a quarter to ten already. Time had passed quickly.

"It only takes five minutes," Tyler said.

"Alright." I stared at the detailed list in front of me. How would I ever remember that? Hopping up, I started unpacking, opening the enormous chifferobe beside my bed. There was more than enough room for my things. My clothes were in decent shape, but they were just sort of basic tops and jeans. Nothing terrible, nothing great. I'd always been happy with them.

I managed to get one of my bags unpacked before Estelle hopped off of her bed. "Let's go," she said brightly.

Tyler twirled her fingers again and the list disappeared. "If you have questions, just ask us. We kind of keep to ourselves. It's okay to hang with any of these groups, but be careful with the vampires and witches." She stared at me solemnly. "They're volatile."

We exited the amazing dorm room and headed downstairs. Our dorms were on the bottom floor. "Is there any rhyme or reason to the dorm assignments?" I asked.

"They mainly gender-sort, but there are a few of us that are non-binary that might not fit in one floor or another, whether by physical difference or internal."

It didn't pass my notice that she included herself. My curiosity had me wondering which category she fit into, but it wasn't my business, so I didn't ask. If she felt like sharing at a later date, she would. In the meantime, she'd introduced herself as female, so that's who she'd be until she told me differently.

"Our first class is PD," Tyler said as she led the way down a flight of stairs I hadn't seen before. "In the basement."

"PD?" I had studied the course catalog but wasn't sure what PD was short for.

"Physical Defense," Estelle said, grabbing the handle of a huge door that opened into a gigantic room full of contraptions for all the physical things we needed to learn. Vampires had to learn how to stalk and attack humans without alerting anyone to their presence. I'd been looking forward to this class. As a half-vampire, I didn't need to feed very often, but when I did, I was ridiculously bad at it. Mom usually helped me.

Shifters, depending on their type, spent a lot of time doing bodybuilding, running, and fighting. It was in their nature.

"What do witches do in this class?" I asked Tyler as we walked around the perimeter of the room.

"Defense magic. Sometimes they'll end up in a literal fight with another paranormal creature or another witch. They have to be able to cast quickly and accurately in the face of danger or attack."

Nodding, I pressed myself against the back wall and watched the other students walk in. Three girls walked in followed by three guys. The one in the front middle, a tiny blonde, flipped her hair behind her shoulders and laughed at something the brunette beside her said. "Who are they?" I asked softly.

"The Sparkles. That one's Kristi Franks. She's basically the queen of the school," Estelle said bitterly. "All the girls want to be her—"

"Not me," Tyler said waspishly.

"And all the guys want to be with her," she finished. "But really, when it comes down to it, everyone hates her."

Watching her walk in, I was struck by how pretty she was, sure, but what really stood out was that everyone in the room turned to watch her enter. Her two friends were pretty too and dressed to the nines. The tiniest one was actually prettier than Kristi. "Who's the brunette?"

Tyler leaned over and whispered as the girls neared. "Sadantha. One of Kristi's Lackeys. Everyone calls her Sadie. She once had the potential to be pretty cool, but Kristi corrupted her. The blonde on Kristi's other side is Madison. She's only accepted into their group because her parents are insanely powerful and wealthy. "

They looked toward the back of the room, but their eyes glanced over us as if we were part of the wall and totally didn't matter. Turning toward the front, they whispered among themselves while the room filled with students.

As they turned, my eyes fell on the three guys that had followed them in. "Who are they?" I whispered, awestruck. They had to be the three hottest guys I'd ever seen in my life.

"Gorgeous, aren't they?" Tyler asked with a wink. "They're the Shifts. Like a hundred years ago, this school was mainly shifters, and that's what they started calling the most athletic. Even though now most of the group is made up of vampires, they still use the name."

Estelle snorted. "Which is odd, because shifters are considered the dredges of the school." She clenched her slight fists. "I wish I could show them a thing or two," she said in a tight voice.

Estelle seemed a bit angry, especially for someone so small. I stood close enough to her now that I could attempt to place her scent. Trying to be discreet, I inhaled slowly and deeply, letting my instincts filter the smells. Ahh, she was a deer of some sort. Maybe antelope. Turning my head to my other side, I tried to do the same with Tyler, but she was more complicated. Some sort of predator, for sure, but what? I'd have to think about it and see if I could place it. I'd smelled it before, I was fairly certain of that.

Returning my gaze to the Shifts, I watched them goof around with each other. All three guys were big, but one of them was gigantic. He had to be nearing seven feet tall.

"The big one got your eye?" Tyler asked with a wink. "That's Jayse." She dropped her voice into a fainter whisper and put her mouth close to my ear. "Lots of us are relatively private about our shifted forms, but literally, nobody knows what he is. He's like the biggest mystery in school. Everyone is dying to know, but nobody can figure it out."

Studying his body movements, I tried to think

about what I'd learned from my parents zoomagology. They studied all manner of shifters as a standard part of their jobs. I couldn't recall any particular shifters being gigantic, except maybe elephants and whales, but elephant scents were distinctive, that wouldn't be a mystery.

"Whale?" I asked softly. "They're usually big and have to live near the ocean."

Estelle shook her head. "No, my cousin Amanda married a whale, I know that smell."

Stumped, I looked at his friends, who were trying to throw a magically enhanced ball over Jayse's head. They weren't successful. He grabbed it every time, but they all enjoyed the effort.

"The short Asian is a witch. Brooks. Everyone says he's got that ancient Chinese black magic, Jincan running through his veins, but he doesn't seem dark to me. Plus, if he was, he'd be hanging with the Noires and doing all kinds of dodgy shit. He was always a loner until they all started playing lacrosse a couple of years back, and then he started hanging with Jayse and Francis." Estelle waved at a kid toward the wall to our left, but I couldn't take my eyes off the guys. The third guy would be Francis, then. He was clearly a vampire. Nobody ever had to tell me when one was around. I could pinpoint every single one in the room, and they undoubtedly could me.

"So that's Francis," I said.

"Yeah, he's Kristi's ex. Bit cocky, but nice enough, usually. All three of them are a little nicer than the rest of the Shifts. The others can get pretty cruel." Tyler's voice took on a sad quality as if she was speaking from experience.

My head was spinning so fast with all the new information the two of them had thrown at me, I didn't even know where to start. Thankfully, I was saved from having to speak by the teacher clapping for attention.

"Split into your usual groups," Coach Cates shouted.

Everyone moved instantly as if that was all they needed to know. I frowned. Well, I needed more than that. Especially if no one seemed to know what I was.

"Excuse me?" I stepped forward, trying to get the teacher's attention.

He turned to me and looked down his nose. This was someone who didn't want to be doing the job he was then. I could always recognize them anywhere.

"What?" he snapped.

"I'm new here..."

He raised an eyebrow. "You're the Davidson girl?" he asked.

I nodded.

"Join the others of your kind and get on with it." He turned away.

"I have two kinds," I whispered, a rock in my gut. I really didn't want to do this in front of the class that was now staring at me.

Behind me, Estelle and Tyler both sucked in a shocked breath. I didn't know how they managed, but my parents somehow managed to keep my hybrid status hidden when I was younger. And since then, they'd just pressed me to never act like a witch or a vampire in social situations. That way, rumors of what I was wouldn't leak out. The vampires would smell me as a vamp, but nobody else would be able to tell.

It seemed that wasn't going to work here.

"Then choose one." He waved me away, going back to his own thoughts and not even attempting to engage with me.

I glanced longingly over at the vampire side just as one of them picked up another and threw them across the room. The body crashed into the wall, and the student slumped down, unconscious.

Right. I was going to be a witch as far as the school was concerned. If my choice was between the two worst cliques, then I was going to go for the one that didn't throw people against the walls.

"See you in a bit," I said to my new friends, shrugging at them before heading over to where a group of mostly girls was hanging out. The guys already seemed to be getting on with what they were supposed to be doing.

The girls threw me looks as I walked closer, and even though it was only a few feet away from me, it felt like the longest walk I'd ever been on.

One of the guys peeled away from the main group and headed in my direction. I mentally prepared myself from the onslaught. I wasn't naive enough to think it wouldn't come, but I'd hoped to have gotten through at least one class without the other students being asses to me.

"Do you need help finding your way around the academy?" he asked, pushing his hand through his hair as he spoke. Not in a suave way, either. He clearly thought he was the hottest guy in the room.

He, in fact, was not.

"I'm all right, but thank you," I answered.

"I can show you all the best hookup spots. The ones even the teachers don't know about." He winked at me. Actually winked. And in that instant, he went from mildly annoying to actually smarmy.

"I don't think so." I hoped he gave up soon, I didn't want to have to hurt him. I was a terrible vampire, but I was still freaking strong *and* a witch.

My dad hadn't been lax with my education all these years, even though Mom said I was hopeless as a vampire.

"Is he bothering you?"

I looked up at the sound of another girl's voice, surprised to find the illustrious Kristi coming towards us, with her cronies in tow.

"Umm..." How was I supposed to respond to that? He obviously was.

I glanced over at where Estelle and Tyler were with the other shifters. Estelle shook her head, warning me off, but it was already too late. Widening my eyes, I shrugged at her. She couldn't help me now.

Kristi put her arm around me and drew me deeper into the gaggle of witches. "Just ignore him. If you don't engage, he's harmless." She walked past him. "Shoo, Zeke. Go find a rock to crawl under."

"Okay..." I wanted to tell her that letting guys like that get away with that sort of repulsive behavior just fed into the culture of boys will be boys, but I figured now probably wasn't the time to point that out. Maybe another time.

From the corner of my eye, I saw Estelle throw her hands up in the air, clearly exasperated with me for having any kind of conversation with Kristi. But I wasn't the kind of person who could easily extract myself from situations like this, especially not when the other person was being nice to me. She'd saved me from the creeper. I'd at least be nice to her.

"Come practice with us. We'll teach you how it goes here." She smiled, the expression not quite reaching her eyes. Maybe she suspected that I'd already been told things about her. Or maybe it was just part of her personality. Some people had dead eyes. It was creepy.

She flicked her long blonde hair over her shoulder. "So, what kind of magic do you have the best affinity for?"

Should I be honest? Tyler had said that nature magic tended to be frowned upon. "I don't really know," I lied. "I've not really tried many."

"If you're a witch, how come you haven't done magic?" Madison asked.

"You can't just ask that," Sadie snapped, acting scandalized.

"No, it's okay. I was home-schooled, so I only learned the magic my parents are best at," I told them.

"Home-schooled? Interesting." Kristi tapped her finger against her chin. "Give us a moment."

"Sure." Not that I had much choice, all three of them had already taken a couple of steps back and talked to one another, completely cutting me out of the conversation. The rest of the class carried on, but I noticed them cutting their eyes in my direction, watching the exchange between the Sparkles and me.

"We're going to let you practice with us now," Kristi said after a couple of minutes of them conspiring. "And for the rest of the week too."

"Oh, thank you." Even I could hear the hesitation in my voice, but I couldn't be rude to her just because of what Estelle said. Nor did I want to be. Plus, Kristi seemed nice. It would be good to have friends at the school from more than one clique. Maybe I could be one of those rare people that clique-hopped.

Madison leaned forward conspiratorially. "On Tuesdays, we do charms." She beamed as she spoke as if she'd just told me the most important piece of information in the world.

I just nodded, at a loss for what else to do. And worried. I didn't know any charms. I just had to hope that Estelle and Tyler had some pointers for me.

"That's not the only rule," Madison continued. "I know it's fun to wear robes in homage to our ancestors, but we only wear them on Fridays, if at all." She wrinkled her nose. "Probably best to just not."

Kristi flipped her hair and looked cooly around the gym, seemingly ignoring her friend's words, but she also didn't contradict her.

"It doesn't matter your affinity. When you're at

school, you sparkle. It's a simple charm. We'll show you."

I didn't have the first clue what she was talking about. "Sparkle?" I knew that was what Estelle and Tyler had called them, but she said it as a verb.

"Look at our auras," Kristi said.

Blinking, I tapped into that part of my vision that let me see auras. I generally didn't prefer to see other people's inner character. It sometimes told too much about a person and swayed my judgment.

Their auras were full of... glitter? I couldn't even tell what they were supposed to look like, or their natural color. "How?" I asked, awestruck. I'd never heard of a spell to change an aura.

"It's just like a glamour. No big deal." Sadie giggled and looped her arm through mine. "We'll get you up to speed in no time."

CHAPTER 3

Estelle laughed maniacally, rolling around on the bed. "They want you to hang out with them?"

"Yes." I frowned. Why was she finding that so hard to believe? I was half-witch, it wasn't that odd that other witches wanted to hang out with me.

"You have to do it," she announced, jumping up. "You can report back to us."

I glanced at Tyler, hoping she'd help convince Estelle that it was a bad idea. She just shrugged.

Great. No back up there.

"I don't know if I can," I said honestly. I had no problem being nice to them, but intentionally being catty was outside my wheelhouse.

"Of course you can," Estelle insisted, calming

down and sitting up. "All you have to do is hang out with them again in PD, and tell us all about it."

"They did seem nice," I started.

"They. Are. Not. Nice," she growled.

"What do you have against them?" This seemed like something more personal than it perhaps should be, and if I was going to do what Estelle wanted me to do, then I needed to know all sides of the story.

"They went to school together and..."

"Tyler!" Estelle warned.

The other girl shook her head.

Right, then. I wasn't going to find out what was going on from them. But maybe if I hung out with Kristi some more, it would come out on its own. Not that I should do that. I'd never had friends before, never mind fake friends.

"I don't think I can do it..."

"Of course you can," Estelle contradicted. She liked to do that. For such a tiny person, she held a lot of force of will. I wondered if it was linked to whatever kind of shifter she was. I didn't know of a forceful deer, though.

"So, you're a witch?" Tyler prompted, her tone revealing the question she really wanted to know.

"Hybrid," I responded. "But no one really knows." I didn't see the point in lying to the two of them. We were going to live in the same dorm for the next three years, at some point, they'd probably see me feed. "I guess the vampires know now. They would've smelled me, then see me join the witches. But they're too much for me."

Tyler whistled loudly. "I've never met one before."

"We're pretty normal." I shrugged. I was just me.

"Have you seen yourself?" Estelle demanded.

"Erm..." Was that a trick question? I knew what I looked like, obviously. But what did that have to do with anything?

Tyler nodded. "Hybrid explains it. All the looks of a witch with the allure of a vampire."

"I don't think..."

"If you want Jayse, you'll have no problem getting him," Tyler promised me.

"Pfft." They were nuts.

"She's right," Estelle promised. "You're hot."

"Erm...thanks?" I didn't know how to respond to any of this. Was it normal for friends to tell each other they were hot? Right now, I was cursing my parents for not sending me to normal school sooner, then I'd have some kind of experience with other people at least.

"So, you'll do it?" Estelle asked, excitement written all over her face.

"Do what?" I'd already forgotten where the conversation had been going, my mind on the three guys I'd seen across the room and the huge one in particular. Jayse had come across like a gentle giant, but that was without me actually talking to him. Maybe once I got to know him and his lacrosse buddies, I'd feel differently and want to stay out of their way.

"Hang out with Kristi and the Sparkles?" Estelle prompted.

I sighed. As far as I could see, there was no way around it. Kristi, no doubt, expected me to say yes to her and spend the week with them. It seemed like no one said no to her, ever. And added to that, Estelle and Tyler now expected me to say yes, too. I was trapped between what my friends wanted and what I wanted.

That wasn't fun.

"I have to get to class," I announced, getting up from my bed and swinging my bag over my shoulder. I didn't want to be late, especially as my next class was botany. I'd been looking forward to this one all day.

"Just think about it."

I sighed. "Fine, I will."

I breathed in the scent of plants and soil, feeling comfortable for the first time since I'd arrived here. This was my affinity. I didn't need any help knowing what to do in this class.

"You must be Tallulah," the teacher said.

"Lou," I corrected her.

"Lou, then. I'm Miss Green, welcome to botany."

I blinked a couple of times. Had she seriously said that her name was Green? When she taught this class?

She chuckled. "Yes, it really is my name. I come from a long line of nature witches and it just stuck."

"Oh." Odd.

"The headmaster said you had an affinity for nature magic?"

I nodded eagerly.

"Good. Your spot is over there with Francis. He'll bring you up to speed. You might want to think about joining the Greenies too. They meet on Wednesdays, and we have a separate room for their plants. We've been blessed enough to receive some very kind donations from wealthy alumni, which means we have some rare plants in there."

My heart skipped a beat. That sounded amazing. "I'll think about it," I said, not wanting to seem too eager even if I wanted to scream my agreement. It might be social suicide to be good at nature magic, but my heart belonged outside.

Instead, I smiled at her before turning and walking towards the empty space next to Francis.

Nerves fluttered in my stomach. He looked perfect, even from afar, and I didn't think I was ready to spend time with him in such close quarters. Estelle had implied that having an affinity for nature magic wasn't cool, what if he thought I was a loser for being good at it? Should I dumb myself down?

"Hi," he said, a wide grin spreading over his face.

"Er...hi." I did an awkward little half-wave as I sat down.

"I don't think we've met."

"Unlikely, as this is my first day," I muttered, overwhelmed by the hotness.

"I'm Francis." He held out his hand and I took it, giving him a firm handshake.

"Lou."

"You smell like vampire."

My eyes widened. What if he'd noticed I'd been hanging out with the witches in PD? My secret could be out within the first day of academy. I'd sort of figured it would be.

"I'm a witch, actually. But I get that a lot," I lied, a slight quiver in my voice. Maybe he'd tell the vampire friends, and I could remain discreet. Hybrids, especially vamp-witch hybrids, were a rare class. I didn't want anyone to think they could take advantage of me. Usually, the offspring of a vampire and witch union turned out entirely vampire or entirely witch.

"Huh, weird." He shrugged. "It's nice to meet you. I hope you're good at this class, I want a good grade." He grinned impishly, sending the nervous butterflies in my stomach crazy.

Or maybe they weren't nervous butterflies at all. Maybe they were something a little bit different from that. Not spending much time with people my own age, I'd never really experienced a crush, but I suspected that was about to change.

It didn't help that he smelled divine, and with every pump of blood around his veins, the smell got stronger, calling to me and begging me to take a bite.

I frowned. Did I need to feed? I'd fed yesterday so I'd be refreshed on my first day, so I shouldn't need to for another week or two. And yet, here I was thinking about Francis' blood like I was starving. Not to mention the odd fact he was a vampire. I shouldn't be craving his blood at all.

I shook my head. Those thoughts and desires needed to disappear. They were only going to distract me from the one class I was actually confident in.

"You all right?" he asked.

"Yes, fine. Sorry. I'm just a little overwhelmed by being in a new place." At least that wasn't completely a lie. Everything seemed so different and intense, and I wasn't entirely sure how to deal with it. I just knew that I needed to get through the day without doing anything stupid.

"Alright class, eyes on the front," Miss Green called.

The chatter died down, which surprised me. If everyone looked down on nature magic, then why would they pay attention in a class like this?

"Today, we're going to be discussing the properties of common garden herbs when it comes to magical cures."

Finally, something I could dig in to. I settled back to see if she knew anything I didn't.

As it turned out, she didn't teach anything I hadn't already learned. It was still interesting.

"Lou, a word?" Ms. Green said as she dismissed class. "Were you bored today?"

"No," I exclaimed. "I enjoyed it."

"But you already knew the material?"

I turned to see if we were alone. Francis waited by

the door. I lowered my voice and leaned in. "Some, but I liked the refresher." Throwing my arms up to show her I was interested, I hit a cup on her desk and it went flying, the contents spraying all over her shirt, which began smoking. She squawked, jerking the shirt off, over her head, as fast as possible.

Just then, Headmaster Schmidt walked into the room, to see Ms. Green stomping on her shirt, her breasts bouncing merrily in a hot pink lacy bra. "What's going on here?" he said quietly.

"Just a little accident," Ms. Green said with a side glance at my horrified face. "Lou spilled some magical weed killer on my shirt."

I turned and looked at Headmaster Schmidt with my mouth gaping. "I didn't mean to," I whispered as I watched Francis' face. It was positively gleeful. Great. He took off, no doubt to tell the whole school what happened.

Ms. Green grabbed a sweater from the back of her chair and put it on. "Can I help you?"

"I just wanted a word about the annual Botany competition and your Greenies involvement." He gave me a severe look. "Don't you have lunch to get to?"

Jumping, I scurried from the room. What a mess. I wasn't even sure where the lunchroom was. As I stood in the hall and looked left to right, an enormous figure turned into the hall and noticed my confusion, even though I turned my face away from him as soon as I saw him. I didn't want him to think I might be staring at him.

"You lost?" Jayse asked from down the hall.

"Maybe a little," I said with a small laugh and half-smile. "Know where the cafeteria is?"

"I'm heading that way myself. Walk with me?"

Now, this was the day looking up. Jayse was possibly hotter than Francis. Maybe. They both had totally different looks but were equally yummy. "Thanks," I said softly as I walked over to him. "It's been a slightly overwhelming day."

"First time at this academy?" he asked.

"At any academy," I said as I reached him. As soon as his scent hit me, I knew. "You're an anaconda?" I asked in surprise.

As Jayse looked at me in surprise, Sadie's earlier words smacked me in the ears. "You can't just ask somebody that."

Asking a shifter about their other form was the height of rudeness unless it was someone very close.

"I'm so sorry," I whispered. "That was so rude."

"Hey, it's no big deal," he said. "But I do try to keep it under wraps. People are really freaked out by snakes."

"I'm not," I said brightly. "My parents are zoomagologists. I've spent a lot of time around snakes and snake shifters. Even wild ones." I nodded at him. "I think you smell nice," I said shyly, turning my head away. What had possessed me to say that? You smell nice? Geez.

"Thanks. So do you. Witch?" He turned a corner, walking slowly as we talked.

"Yeah." I knew his secret, so it would only be fair to tell him mine, but I kept my mouth shut. I didn't want him to blab all over school. I didn't know him well enough yet.

"Well, here it is. I'm going to go sit with the other Shifts. See you in class." He smiled down at me then lumbered off toward the table full of his friends. I got in line. When my tray was loaded with surprisingly yummy-looking food, I looked around the cafeteria, but couldn't find Tyler and Estelle anywhere. Maybe they'd already eaten. Walking around the perimeter of the lunchroom, I avoided the table full of Jayse, Francis and their friends. I didn't even see the Sparkles. I would've gladly sat with them to avoid this awkwardness. Everyone turned away from me as I passed their tables as if they were hoping I wouldn't ask to sit with them.

With a sigh, I left the lunchroom, stepping out a side door. It opened into a small rooftop patio that faced the water. Three picnic tables sat empty. I wondered what was wrong with the patio as I sat down and ate. At least I was outside. My energy recharged as I nibbled on the food, but I was absorbing magic from nature more than getting energy from food. The sun, the salty air, it was all good for me. As a hybrid, I needed to connect with my affinity, drink blood, and eat food in order to remain healthy and whole.

Even though I felt better having sat outside for a while, it was still a lonely lunch. Maybe I could figure out when Estelle and Tyler ate and sit with them the next day.

My last class of the day was a double period of human studies. The paranormal world and the human world was kept carefully separate. It wasn't easy, with magical creatures running around and rogue paranormals that had to be controlled, but it was necessary. Humans always reacted badly when they found out about us. It had happened before and took a massive amount of magic to fix. That was part of my mom's new job at the zoo. The humans thought she was just a janitor, cleaning the zoo overnight. But in reality, she worked for the National Society of Zoomagologists. They had someone at every zoo, watching out for magical animals. Most zoos also had a secret branch unknown to humans, but this one didn't, yet. Mom was slated to open it up.

"Psst." I looked around to see who was making that noise. Ah, finally. Tyler sat in the back of the classroom, waving eagerly.

As I turned to sit with her, Kristi spotted me. "Lou. Over here." She was in the front far side of the room, opposite of Tyler. I shrugged at my friend and joined the Sparkles.

"This is the worst class." Madison groaned. "Why do we need to know this stuff, anyway?"

"My mom and dad use it a lot," I said. "It can be pretty interesting."

Kristi looked down her nose at me. "Madison doesn't have a need to learn anything like this. Her father invented the Magi-Wave." With a hair flip, she dismissed us both. I was a little impressed, though. Even we had a Magi-Wave. All you had to do was select the recipe on the screen and put the raw ingredients into it, and it could prepare over a hundred meals. "Anyway," Kristi continued. "You should come back to our dorm with us after class and hang."

She said it with a finality that gave me no room to argue. "Okay, then," I said softly as the teacher walked to the front of the class.

Francis, Jayse, and their other friend, Brooks,

walked in just as the teacher opened his mouth. "Find a seat, boys," the slight man said.

They sat on the opposite side of the room but looked our way. Kristi gave them a little finger wave, which Francis returned. So, they were still friendly. I probably never stood a chance anyway.

The class was boring. Madison was half right. They'd wasted an opportunity to take an interesting class and gave it to the world's most monotone teacher. Even I found myself fighting sleepy eyes halfway through.

Madison slipped a note onto my desk, pulling me from my stupor.

Madison: I heard you walked to lunch with Jayse.

I scribbled a reply and handed it back.

Me: Yeah, why?

She handed it back fast.

Madison: He's super hot!

I giggled and looked back at her. She was looking over at Jayse and his friends wiggling her eyebrows up and down.

"Ladies, would you like to share something with the class?"

"No, sir," we said in innocent unison.

We nearly dissolved into giggles again since we'd spoken the same words, at the same time, in the same intonation. Kristi looked back at us with an eyebrow raised. "If you're going to share a brain get one that works," she hissed, then flipped her hair.

Her words didn't bother me, I knew I was smart. But when I glanced back at Madison, she was crushed, and Sadie looked upset beside her.

I didn't say anything else to them until class was over. Finally, my first day was done. It had been awkward and difficult. And I still had to go to Kristi's room.

"Let's go," she said, starting off. As she passed Francis, she smiled coyly. "Hey, Francis."

He barely looked away from Brooks as he replied. "Oh, hey Kristi."

"Are you going to practice?" she asked.

Francis, Brooks, and Jayse turned to face us. "Of course." He raised his eyebrows. Maybe he wasn't as into her as she was him. "Hey, Lou," he said.

Jayse echoed him. "Hey, Lou, what's up? This is our friend Brooks."

I nodded at them and smiled shyly, tucking my hair behind my ear. "Nice to meet you," I said.

"You, too." They grabbed their bags and walked out the door. Kristi waited for them to leave the room before turning to me. "You already know Francis and Jayse?"

"Not really. I have Botany with Francis, and Jayse showed me the way to the cafeteria."

She pursed her lips. "They're great guys. Come on."

We didn't talk as we followed her through the halls. Walking behind her was a new experience for me. Her head was held high, and somehow, maybe she had a spell on, but everyone just moved out of her way. She didn't have to say excuse me, or squeeze between two people, or wait for someone to move. She just walked, her Sparkles to her immediate left and right, and me in their wake.

Without having to stop every five feet to maneuver the crowded hall, we made it to her dorm in no time.

It was hot pink. The whole thing. Each shade of pink complemented the other, in some pink-matching miracle of decorating. As nauseating as it was, it worked.

She threw open her big wardrobe and surveyed the contents. As I looked around, I realized there was only one bed in the room. "You don't share a room?" I asked. There were three of the same chiffarobes that I had in my room with Estelle and Tyler, but just the one bed.

"No, my mom made sure I had my own." She sniffed and moved to the next, throwing open the doors. "I have nothing to wear. We need to go shopping."

After seeing some of the styles in the school, I really wouldn't have minded doing a little shopping myself. My parents gave me an allowance for such things, but I'd never spent much. When I was off with them, traveling around the world, I hadn't really needed an extensive wardrobe.

CHAPTER 4

The mall was bigger than I expected and full of humans, totally throwing me off. I'd not spent much time around humans.

"Are we okay being here?" I asked.

"Why wouldn't we be?" Sadie answered.

"It's just, not on campus..." And I'd read the rules, which had said something about needing permission to leave the grounds. Plus, all the humans.

She shrugged like it wasn't important. "We're over eighteen, they can't do anything to us."

"We could get expelled." Nerves fluttered in my stomach as I brought that up. I didn't like being the person throwing a kink in the works, but I didn't want to disappoint my parents, and I knew the academy was pricey. It was only because they'd been saving my whole life that I'd even been able to attend.

"And lose our money? They wouldn't dare." Kristi barely even looked behind her as she spoke, clearly not at all as worried as me about getting caught.

"Alright, then." I should have expected this when they'd said we were going shopping, but naively, I'd thought there'd be some way of doing that without leaving school grounds and breaking the rules.

I just had to hope that the whole strict rules thing wasn't quite the case. I had to wonder what everyone else did that broke the rules, but I guessed I'd find out as time went by.

"Do many people come here?" I asked.

"All the time," Madison answered, bouncing along as if she wasn't wearing high heels. I hoped I wouldn't be expected to do the same. I was more of a barefoot kind of girl than one that spent a lot of time trying to balance on a thin point.

"Okay. Where to first?"

"We need to hit up the shoe store first, we can't have you going around in those," Kristi said, glancing down at my sneakers.

I wanted to ask what was wrong with them, but I knew already. They'd already explained a lot of things, like how I had to wear certain colors on certain days, or how I had to wear my hair. It gave me a headache just thinking about it, but I knew there was no other way if I wanted to keep hanging out with them.

And even though it hadn't been long, I knew I didn't have much choice in the matter. Even if Estelle hadn't wanted me to keep hanging out with the Sparkles, I wouldn't be able to just leave without them making my life hell.

"Oh, I need to go to Snip and Blow." Sadie flicked her hair, an action I'd seen all three of them do multiple times. It seemed unlikely that it was a natural habit, then. More a learned one. No doubt I'd need to use it too if I was to become one of them.

"Take Lou with you. She could use a bit of shaping," Kristi instructed.

It was easy to tell who was in charge here. *And* that the other two just went along with it.

I started to protest but shut my mouth when I thought better of it. "What's Snip and Blow?" I asked instead.

"The hairdresser," Sadie responded. "The best one around. I've never met anyone who was able to tame this disaster zone quite so well." She pats her sleek dark hair. "Not even with magic."

"It looks beautiful." And it did. The light bounced off it and shined in a way that made me wish I wasn't ice blonde.

"Not when it doesn't get regular treatment."

"Oh." I didn't know what to say to that. I also wasn't completely sure I wanted to let anyone touch my hair, though I supposed I could use magic to put it back to normal if they made a mess of it.

"But the shoes first. The hair can wait." Kristi headed to the left and into a shop that really was full of shoes. Every wall had shelves and shelves of heels, and all of them looked expensive and uncomfortable.

I was going to make Estelle pay for this. I wasn't this kind of girl and had no real desire to be. But if it was part of the cost of hanging out with Kristi and the Sparkles, then I'd have to take it. At least I had plenty of money in my account.

Yay, past me. Bye, bye savings.

"Oh, these would look amazing!" Sadie passed me a pair of wedges with emerald green straps on them before leaning in close. "If you're not used to heels, these'll be easier to walk in," she whispered, all the time watching for where Kristi was.

No doubt the head Sparkle wouldn't want me wearing something comfortable, but I appreciated Sadie's help, remembering what Estelle had said about her being nice, just corrupted.

"Thanks."

"Those won't do," Kristi sneered, pushing the

wedges out of the way and replacing them with a pair of completely impractical white strappy heels.

"Aren't these more for formal events?" I asked, looking at them warily. How would they even stay on my feet?

"Only if you're over forty. Put them on and walk."

Seeing no other choice, I kicked off my socks and sneakers and started wrestling with the thin straps of the horrible shoes. I already hated the things, and I hadn't even tried wearing them yet.

Kristi tutted, but I tried not to focus on her too much. I should start thinking about taking my nice assessment back. She had all the makings of a bitch, especially if she was going to do things like insist I wore these damn shoes. Her niceness had been superficial. The more I got to know her, the more the bitch came out.

Finally getting them buckled, I rose to my feet, all of my attention going to staying balanced. I pulled on my vampire side, hoping the speed and elegance that were ingrained in me would kick in and let me walk without harming myself. I might not have been good at feeding, but the other parts of being a vampire, I didn't do too badly at.

"Not bad," Kristi said, looking me up and down with a disdainful eye. "But we need to get you some new clothes, too. Buy the shoes I left behind the counter, then we'll go to the next store."

The moment she headed toward the door, I rolled my eyes. It seemed like this trip was going to be expensive, even if I didn't want it to be.

Estelle laughed the moment I walked through the door. Her laughing at me was starting to become a regular occurrence, and it was going to get on my nerves.

"What did they do to you? she asked through the laughter.

"Gave me a makeover," I mumbled as I dropped my bags next to the bed. I didn't want to add up what I'd spent and was very grateful that my parents wouldn't check in on my account, or else they'd have some questions about what I was doing with my time.

"You look like a baby prostitute," she said.

"Thanks." I sat down on my bed and wrestled with the stupid strappy shoes. I hated them with a passion.

"I'm serious..."

"I know." I rolled my eyes. "But you wanted me to

hang out with them, so I did. This is a consequence of that."

"But they still want you to hang out with them?" She perked up, her laughter fading.

"Yes, they seem to like me. Though they said something about a Sparkle Charm that I need to use, they haven't taught it to me yet." I rubbed my forehead, already worrying that I wasn't going to be able to keep up the charade long enough. "Do either of you know it?"

"No," Estelle barked.

"Yes."

I turned to Tyler, an odd expression on my face as I focused on her smell. I still couldn't get a proper read on her, which was unusual. I'd even managed with Jayse, and everyone had said that he was a mystery. It just made no sense that she didn't have a distinct one.

"Can you teach me?" I tried not to let the hope enter my voice, but I couldn't help it. There was too much riding on me being able to do this. I didn't want to risk getting kicked out of the Sparkles so soon. Madison and Sadie might let me drift away without revenge, but Kristi would surely make me miserable.

"Sure." She shrugged. "It's an easy one."

"That's because you know it," I muttered. No one

was making life easy for me here, that was for certain. Why did everything have to be quite so cloak and dagger? It wasn't like we were all part of some kind of secret society or anything.

"Do you know how to tap into your aura?" she asked.

I nodded. That was being a paranormal one-oh-one. Most people learned to do it as a child. Though from what I'd heard, a lot of shifters never actually bothered. They didn't think they needed it when they already had an alternative animal form.

"Slip into your aura," she instructed.

I took a deep breath and closed my eyes, doing what she said, letting the scent of freshly turned soil and cherry-tomato vines overtake me. This was how I smelled to myself. I didn't fully understand auras, but as far as I was aware, they had something to do with what the paranormal believed was their inner center. And mine was green. Everywhere.

"Raise your hands..."

I did, feeling like a bit of an idiot, but doing it anyway.

"And repeat after me..."

I cleared my throat, getting ready to say whatever rhyme was needed to make the charm work. Magic wasn't something that followed a set of strict rules. Some things needed rhymes, and some things just became as naturally as a click of the fingers. Apparently, this was the former.

"Sprinkle, sparkle, glitter, gloop..."

"Sprinkle, sparkle, glitter, gloop," I repeated, trying not to let myself laugh at the ridiculous words. Whoever had created that one hadn't been very creative.

"Show the glitter, bibbity boop."

"Show the glitter, bibbity boop." I opened my eyes, knowing that she was finished even if she didn't explicitly say it. "Is that really it, or are you pulling my leg?" I asked, feeling a little silly for actually repeating the words.

"Those are the real words," she promised. "Look at my aura if you don't believe me."

I frowned. Look at her aura? I knew that shifters had them, but I didn't realize they could use charms the same way as...

I sucked in a sharp breath and opened my mouth to ask the question I already knew the answer to, but Tyler shook her head. Huh. She didn't want to be outed as hybrid then? That made sense, I'd have kept it quiet if I could have. I hadn't even considered it when she'd done the spell to control the pen, but she definitely smelled like a shifter.

Instead, I did what she asked and looked at her aura, seeing the sparkles there.

"Does it bother you that they still use your original charm?" Estelle asked from the bed.

Interesting. She knew that Tyler could influence her aura, but didn't know why. I thought the two of them were as thick as thieves, but apparently not.

"I'm over it," Tyler responded. "And to answer your question about the words, I made it when I was eight," she said with a shrug.

"Oh."

I didn't say it out loud, but I was impressed. Not many people were able to create charms at such a young age. I didn't think I'd even tried at that age. My first one had been at fifteen when I'd wanted to make a color-changing streak in my hair.

What I wouldn't give for something so individual now. But I doubted it would fit with the Sparkles strict dress code.

"Thank you," I said, realizing that I should have started with that one. I didn't want her to think that I was ungrateful for the help she was giving. "So, what do we do now?" I'd eaten dinner while out with the Sparkles, which didn't leave a lot to do for the evening, especially as none of our classes had really given us homework. Apparently, that was something they saved for a couple of weeks into the term.

"We can play cards if you want? Or stick a movie

on." Tyler shrugged. "No one will check on us, so we can pretty much do anything we want."

"That seems to be a theme here," I murmured.

Estelle scoffed. "Tell me about it. They like to give us all these rules like we're kids, but then they just leave us be and never enforce them. They don't even have proper detention here."

"Then what's the point of the rules at all?"

"Self-enforcement? There are always some people who will want to stick to all of them, and they'll pressure the others into obeying. It works for the most part," Tyler said.

"Huh." I supposed that was true. I'd had rules at home and mostly kept to them because I wanted to, rather than fearing the consequences if I didn't. My parents weren't the sort to need the punishment angle to keep me in line.

"Cards?" Tyler asked.

"Sure, teach me the rules?" I beamed at her, feeling more relaxed than I had my entire afternoon with the Sparkles. These were definitely the people I wanted to be my friends. Laidback and natural. I planned to make the most of it.

CHAPTER 5

We only had PD on Mondays, Tuesdays, and Thursdays, so Wednesday's first class was Botany. I took a few extra minutes getting ready without really knowing why. I found myself bugged by one curl at the end of my blonde hair that wouldn't flip to the right, only the left.

"Ack," I said, exasperated. I'd still not put on much makeup, not really knowing how to apply it. They'd made me buy some at the mall, but I'd only used the mascara and some lip gloss.

"What's wrong?" Estelle asked.

"This one curl won't turn right," I grumbled. "But it's stupid, I shouldn't even be worried about it. I normally don't curl my hair at all, but I can't wear a ponytail."

"Use a glamour," she suggested as she looked over my shoulder into the mirror. "I'm not sure how. Tyler, do you know?"

"Yep," Tyler said. "I used to do them a lot."

Oh, I hardcore wanted to ask why, but like with her hybrid status and the smell I couldn't pinpoint, I felt like it would be an intrusion to our friendship for me to push. "Can you show me?"

"They're super simple. Do you know how to pool your magic in your hand?"

"Of course." I'd been taught as a toddler. Some spells required a magic washing, so to speak. Covering an object in magic and imbibing it with intent made it change, move, etc. Ohhhh, I understood.

"I think I know what to do." I pooled the magic in my hand and smoothed the curl, telling my magic what I wanted it to do. It curled perfectly.

"There you go!" Tyler said. "Great job. Try something harder?"

"I would, but I've got to go to class. Thanks for helping me!" I grabbed my bag and hightailed it out of the dorm room. They had both taken Botany in the fall semester when I was still homeschooled, so they had an independent study period while I'd be in class with hot Francis. Too bad he was totally off-limits.

Sliding into the classroom just in time, I took my

seat beside Francis again. "Hey, new kid," he said with a wink.

"Oh, great, I get a cool nickname."

"It could be worse," he whispered as Ms. Green stood. "It could be booger-face, or big toe or something."

"Big toe?" I asked with a laugh.

He shrugged and turned around as Ms. Green stared pointedly at us. "Now that everyone is paying attention," she said. "We're continuing the lesson from yesterday. Everyone kindly go grab a garden plant from the back of the room."

Frances walked really close behind me as we moved to the back of the room to the table. Plants were growing all over the large room, but the table was full of things even most humans grew in their home gardens.

"As we get into bigger and more dangerous plants and spells, we'll move our classes to the greenhouses, but I like to start in here while we get to know each other," Ms. Green said as I selected a healthy-looking growth of oregano. I loved the smell.

"You look like you're taking this seriously," Francis said in a whisper as he randomly grabbed a plant.

"I am," I said without thinking. He chuckled, then I remembered that it was supposed to be super bad to like botany. "I mean, I can't have something that stinks." Flipping my hair just like the Sparkles, I turned and walked back to my seat, my step steadier than it had been the day before in the heels. Maybe it got easier the longer I wore them.

I hadn't been able to bring myself to wear the white heels to class. Kristi had put some stiletto pumps behind the counter for me to buy, so I'd worn them with my narrow-legged jeans and a new black shirt. I liked the way my blonde hair looked against the dark material.

With a sway of my hips, I sat down, sure Francis's eyes were on me. The power of that knowledge felt pretty damn good. Ms. Green gave us instructions for the best ways to cut the plants to get the maximum benefit in spells. I already knew, of course, and had mine cut into a small pile in no time.

"Great job, Lou," Ms. Green said. "Maybe you can show Francis."

I turned to see him with a huge pile of greenery on his desk. He shrugged sheepishly. "I'm no good with a knife. I'm not even good with them in PD class. Can't be good at everything, right?"

Grabbing my knife, I took another sprig of his mint and showed him the proper angle to cut. "If you cut on its lifelines, it'll give you more power in your potions and spells."

He watched carefully, then tried himself, totally messing it up. "I told you, I'm hopeless."

I laughed and showed him again, but gave up quickly. He wasn't interested at all.

"Thanks for not telling the whole school about me burning up Ms. Green's shirt," I said softly. "I appreciate it."

"I mean, it was hilarious," he said. "And I did tell Brooks and Jayse. But other than that, nobody needed to know."

Smiling, I continued cutting. He was kinder than I'd expected him to be, considering he was Kristi's ex.

"So, are you coming Friday?" he asked.

"To what?" I had no idea what was going on Friday.

"The dorm party," he said simply. Apparently, I should've already known what he was talking about.

"Oh, I didn't know about it."

"The Shifts are hosting a huge party in our dorm. Friday at six."

"But isn't there some big rule about girls and guys not going into each other's dorms?" I'd already broken some pretty major rules. I didn't want to get busted and kicked out of school.

"Eh, the teachers mostly go home on Fridays. The

few that stay bury themselves in their rooms. We can do whatever."

Nobody seemed too concerned about the rules. I guessed it wasn't such a big deal as the headmaster had tried to make out.

As we packed up our plants and tools at the end of class, Francis asked me again. "So, are you coming?"

Trying to be totally casual, I shrugged at him with a half-smile. "I might come around to see how it is."

"Great." His smile was freaking killer. "I'll see you there."

The urge to lean over and sink my teeth into his neck overwhelmed me again. What the heck? Vampires didn't typically bite each other. Maybe during sex, but that was all. Why would I want to bite him so badly?

To my relief, the bell rang, pushing the thought from my head.

I pushed the stew around my bowl, pulling a face at it and trying not to let the grayness of it put me off.

"Never get the stew," Kristi warned me. "I don't know what they do to it, but that stuff is vile."

"I'm starting to realize that," I responded, trying

not to let my glumness seep over into my voice. None of which was helped by the pinching in my toes and the tightness of my shirt. I'd never felt so self-conscious in my life, and I didn't like it, despite my feelings on the contrast between my hair and blouse. How the three of them went about their days without having to worry about how they looked was beyond me. But I had to act the part.

I glanced over at where Estelle and Tyler sat, longing to be with them. When it came to the two other girls, there was no effort needed in being myself.

And yet, I had to admit I liked the attention that Kristi and the others paid to me. They wanted me to fit in and did what they could to make that happen. The two parts of myself were almost at war inside me. And I didn't mean my vampire and witch sides, they were coasting along like normal. I'd never really thought about my dual natures as much until I came here.

"Lou? Are you listening to me?" There was an edge of a threat in Kristi's voice.

"Sorry, I was lost in thought." I smiled at her but could tell from the set of her lips and the daggers in her eyes that she wasn't impressed with me.

"I was saying that I want to lose weight before the

Spring formal." She looked around at the three of us, her gaze full of expectation.

Both Sadie and Madison caught on quicker than I did and started gushing about how she didn't need it. One look at her told me they were right. If anything, she was too skinny, but that was an opinion I kept to myself. It wasn't worth the headache I'd receive in return.

"You don't need to," I added in, completely unnecessarily. The other two were doing enough placating for all of us combined.

"Whatever. I want some fries." She scraped back her chair and walked over to the counter, leaving the rest of us behind.

"So, have you met any cute guys yet?" Sadie asked, leaning across the table with her whole attention on me.

Madison follows suit, waiting for me to answer.

"Jayse is pretty hot," I admitted.

They nodded eagerly, probably because every girl at the academy thought the same.

"And there's Francis, he's in my botany class..." His flirtations from the morning made me blush.

"Lou. You can't like him," Sadie cut in frantically.

"Oh, my gosh, no." Madison shook her head as she echoed her friend's sentiments.

"Why not?" I frowned. I hadn't really planned on

dating anyone, but I didn't like the implication that I couldn't. That just seemed unfair.

"He's Kristi's ex. That makes him forbidden."

"Oh." Now she said it, I remembered Estelle telling me that too, I just hadn't thought it was particularly important at the time. Apparently, I was wrong.

"You're lucky we asked," Sadie assured me with wide eyes. "We wouldn't have wanted you to get into that much trouble." There was a note of something real beneath her words. Almost like she was actually looking out for me, rather than just listening to the list of crazy rules the Sparkles had. Was she really that scared of Kristi?

I was about to ask her for more information when Kristi returned, slamming down her plate of fries, smothered in ketchup and mayonnaise. Just looking at it turned my stomach, but if that was what she was going to eat, then it wasn't on me to judge. The fries were fine, but the mound of condiments on top was too much.

"Are fries part of your diet?" Madison asked before being shushed by Sadie.

"What do I care? Even if I put the weight on I can glamour it away. You know that," Kristi snapped.

"Glamour it?" My question slipped out before I

meant it to, but my curiosity had gotten the better of me. I hadn't realized weight could be glamoured.

"Do you not know about glamouring?" Kristi asked, leaning back in her chair. "How interesting."

"It's not something I've ever really done," I said. My first glamour had just been that morning when Tyler helped me with the curl in my hair, so it was just a small lie.

"We'll teach you," she promised. She looked me over. "I thought for sure you were using a glamour spell." She sniffed and returned to her fries.

Had she just insulted me? Or was it a backhanded compliment? I wasn't at all sure. "Thanks." But I remembered how little effort they'd made to teach me the Sparkle charm. It was almost as if that had actually been a test of sorts to see if I would manage to pass. I was glad I'd thought to ask Tyler about it, otherwise, I might have ended up booted out of the Sparkles.

And there I went again. I actually did want their approval, even though my dorm mates disliked them. Kristi definitely had her moments of being a bitch, but all of them had been nice to me so far, giving me the advice and help I needed to fit into the school.

"What are you wearing to the party tomorrow

night?" Sadie asked. "I was thinking of the little black number with the red mesh..."

"You can't wear that. Mesh is my thing," Kristi cut in. "Wear the green skater dress with the halter top."

Sadie glanced away, but not before I caught the hurt in her eyes.

"Is that the one you bought the other day? It looked super cute," I told her, hoping it would pick her up. Luckily, I seemed to have judged it right, and a smile lit up her face.

"Yes, that's the one."

"It looked great," I assured her.

"What about you, Lou? What are you going to wear?" Kristi asked.

"I'm not sure yet, but I'll find something." My first thought when Francis had invited me to the party was that I'd get to spend time with him. It hadn't been what I was going to wear. I was a terrible Sparkle, clearly.

"Don't forget you still need to abide by the rules," Kristi reminded me. "No blue on Fridays." A smirk twisted her lips even as she sipped from her soda.

The bitch. She knew the fanciest thing I owned was the blue sequined dress I'd bought while we were out shopping the other day. And now she was implying that I couldn't wear it. She just longed to make people unhappy. Or just look inferior to her.

The idea that I had to keep pretending to like her was starting to grate. At first, she'd been somewhat fun to be around, but the more I was with her, the more I wanted to be away from her.

"We could go shopping after class if you want?" Sadie suggested, clearly trying to rescue me like I had her.

"No can do. I have an appointment," Kristi said, smirking all the more.

Madison groaned. "But without your car, we can't get into town."

"Sorry." Kristi didn't even wait for us to protest more. Instead, she rose to her feet and flicked her hair over her shoulder. "Talk to you all later." She gave us a sarcastic wave.

I narrowed my eyes. She thought she was being so careful with keeping us in line, but I saw it for what it really was. She was insecure and needed to keep us down. What was most interesting to me was that Sadie and Madison really didn't seem to be anywhere near as malicious.

"You can come to our dorm tonight and see if I have anything that'll fit you?" Sadie suggested.

"You two bunk together?" It made sense, but so far, I'd only seen Kristi's room.

"Yes. Just the two of us. We're lucky," Sadie said.

"Who are you bunked with?" Madison added.

She'd been quiet, but that seemed like her personality. Maybe she'd just been recruited by Kristi for reasons other than who she was. Estelle had said she'd come from a powerful family.

"I don't know their names," I lied. "They seem like weirdos." I cringed inwardly at referring to my friends like that, but I wasn't convinced that telling the truth would win me any points in this situation.

"I'm so sorry," Madison said, her eyes wide and concerned for me.

"We can see if we can get you transferred to our room," Sadie promised.

"You really don't have to..."

She waved away my concern. "Don't worry about it, my father's the inventor of the Magi-Wave, I can get what I want."

"Well, we'll talk about that later. I'm not worried, you guys are great." I wasn't just saying that. They were trying hard to help me.

CHAPTER 6

Even though the two of them had invited me here, I still felt nervous about going there. What if they'd changed their minds? Or if Kristi had got to them. I wasn't naive enough to think that this would sit well with the head Sparkle. She wanted all three of us to fall in line, and meeting up without her certainly wasn't that.

I lifted my fist and rapped a couple of times on the door.

It swung open straight away, revealing Sadie on the other side with her hair up in a ponytail.

I raised my eyebrow.

"Come in, you don't have to knock," she said ushering my inside and glancing up and down the corridor.

Okie dokie then. I wasn't wrong about Kristi not being okay with this meetup. Interesting.

"Don't tell," she whispered, clearly fearing I'd reveal the terrible faux-pas of wearing her hair up to the world.

"Of course not," I promised, I was tempted to dig a hair tie out of my bag and put my own hair up. I would've been far more comfortable with it out of the way.

The room was a lot less lavish than Kristi's, with the normal three bed set up, though from what they'd said, no one else slept here with them. That was probably a good thing if Sadie was going to break the Sparkle rules.

"Let me pull a few options out of my closet," she bubbled, striding over to the overflowing piece of furniture. That was some collection of clothing she had there.

I wandered around the room, trying not to disturb Madison who was lying on her bed with earbuds in, silently mouthing the words to a song. I wasn't sure what she was doing, but it looked pretty involved.

"Don't mind her," Sadie said. "Her affinity is to music-based magic."

"That's a thing?"

"Anything is." She threw a dress on the bed. "If a

concept exists, there's some witch out there who has an affinity for it. Personally, I think that's where the legends about things like sirens and succubi came from. They're not actually real, just witches with affinities for music and sex."

I glanced at Madison, starting to see her in a new light. "What about you?" I asked.

"You can't just ask what someone's affinity is, you know?"

I'd have been worried if I hadn't been able to hear the amusement in her voice.

"The sea," she answered with a shrug. "I'm actually the heir to one of the sea covens."

"You are?" I stopped running my fingers down the spines of the books on their shelf as I turned to look at her.

"Just...don't tell anyone," she said with a hint of bitterness. "Kristi doesn't like it if people remember I have more power than she does." Her eyes widened and her hand flew to her mouth.

"I won't tell anyone," I said quickly.

"Thank you. I didn't actually mean it. Well, I did. But I don't. It's so confusing," she babbled, losing the facade of confidence she'd had since the moment we'd all met.

"Is that why we're not able to wear blue on Fridays?" I turned back to the books, trying to make it seem as if there was nothing important in the question, even if I thought I knew the answer.

"Yes," she whispered. "Fridays are sacred to my coven and one of our traditions is to wear blue."

I'd read that. It was a common religious theme with sea witches, the color blue. "Then why does she stop you?" I looked back at her, intrigued to see her reaction.

She shrugged. "Maybe it's a reminder. Perhaps she looks bad in blue."

I snorted. That sounded about right.

My finger caught on one of the books, and I felt an unknown pull towards that particular one. I hadn't felt that when I'd touched any of the others. I tugged it from the shelf and tried to make sense of what I was looking at from the cover. The supple purple leather was brighter than it should be, but that was probably something to do with the golden runes decorating the front of it.

Slowly, I opened it up, not at all surprised to find the heavy parchment inside it. No matter what this book was about, the thing was old.

Each page had hundreds of teeny hand-scribbled notes on it, both in ink and in something that looked suspiciously like blood. A memory of a haggard old witch writing in blood sprang to mind, but I pushed it to the side. That couldn't be linked to this. Not when it was in the possession of a sea witch.

"What is this?" I asked, deciding that it was worth a shot. She'd answered all my other questions so far, there was no reason to think she wouldn't answer this one.

I held it out so she could see what I was talking about.

Sadie sucked in a deep breath, somehow raising Madison from her odd trance-like state.

"That's Kristi's," she announced. "She wanted us to keep it for her so she didn't get caught with it."

I frowned. That seemed like an awful thing for someone to do to their friends.

"What does it do?" I hoped it had nothing to do with the old woman I'd encountered in Africa. The moment my parents had discovered there was a blood witch around, they'd pulled out of the research mission they'd been part of and we'd flown straight back to our home base. It was the one and only time they'd abandoned a chance to learn, and a little part of me had always wondered why they'd done it.

Maybe I was about to understand.

"We don't really know," Madison admitted.

"She asked you to hide something, but didn't tell you what it was?" This was sounding shadier by the second. It was a good thing I didn't really trust her to start with.

"Not quite. She claimed that if you write in it in blood, then whatever you write comes true. I've never tried it though. We wrote some stuff in pen a couple of times..." She trailed off and glanced away.

"What happened?" Now my curiosity really was piqued. What could that book do? A worried part of me suspected I was right to draw parallels between the witch in Africa and what Sadie was saying about this book.

Something about it certainly wasn't right. Even just holding it in my hands made me feel uncomfortable, potentially because the part of me that was completely entrenched in nature was rebelling against something that broke the rules of it.

One thing was for certain, I'd never use this horrible book.

"The things we wrote became rumors," Madison admitted. "We didn't know if it had anything to do with what we wrote, but it happened three times. We vowed never to use it again unless Kristi outright told us to."

The two girls shared uneasy glances as if wondering if I was also going to make them use it.

"I think that's a good idea." I shut the book and

slipped it back onto the shelf, not wanting any more to do with it. "But why not destroy it?"

"And tell Kristi what?" Sadie asked bitterly. "She comes to use it sometimes. Or asks us to bring it to her. If we suddenly couldn't produce it, then I don't know what would happen."

"We're not even sure it can be destroyed." Madison didn't seem at all thrilled by the idea of that.

"Oh." There had to be a way. My dad would know, but then Madison and Sadie would get blamed for its loss.

"But let's stop talking about it. We can't change what we have no control over. We *can* change what you're wearing on Friday night though. Come see the choices." She waved at the dresses on the bed.

I nervously made my way over, my heels clicking on the floor.

"Oh!" She disappeared back to her closet and pulled out a pair of fluffy slippers. "So you can rest your feet now," she assured me.

I groaned in actual relief, stepping out of my shoes and into the comfy slippers. "Thanks, you have no idea how amazing they feel right now."

Sadie chuckled. "Believe me, I do. There's no better feeling than taking your heels off after a long day and putting soft, cushy shoes on."

"Maybe not wearing the heels in the first place," I muttered.

She chuckled. "There are limits to what I can risk," she said cryptically.

"Alright, so these are the options. Personally, I think you want the long-sleeved velvet maroon skater. The dark red will look great with your hair if you do it in ringlets again, and you can wear your black pumps with it too if you're not feeling up to the strappy white ones." She pointed to the dress in question, one that I had to admit was beautiful. "And," she said excitedly as she held it up, "It's backless."

The fabric shone in the light of the torches, and I longed to lean down and stroke it.

"Oh, but what about the mini dress with the sheer maxi skirt?" Madison asked, finally getting off her bed and joining us. "Lou's got great legs, that one would look awesome."

"Hmm. That's a good point," Sadie said, tapping a finger against her chin. "And you did say that you thought Jayse was hot. He'd like something that made you look taller..."

I opened my mouth to protest but closed it again. Jayse *was* hot. Maybe even hotter than Francis was, though I didn't like choosing between them. I might not have come here for my love life, but that didn't mean I had to ignore it.

"Alright, yes. Let's dress to impress," I announced.

The two of them giggled, clearly happy that I was coming around to their way of thinking. I had to admit that having girlfriends like this was kind of fun. Way more so than I expected. And I was going to make the most of it.

CHAPTER 7

"Damn," I said as I finished my hair. No need for a glamour on it this morning, it had curled properly. "I forgot we have PD this morning."

I'd dressed all wrong for PD. "Is there a spell to actually change my clothes, not just glamour them different?" I asked. "I shouldn't have worn a dress and heels for PD."

"No time now," Tyler said as she tied her sneakers. "Let's go."

I took another second to grab a bag and stuff leggings and a tee into it, along with socks. Snatching up my sneakers from the bottom of my wardrobe, I ran after them. Halfway down the hall, I realized I'd left my regular backpack, so I had to double back.

The locker rooms for PD were just outside the

gym. Peeking into the gym, I sighed. It looked like everyone was there. This was only my second PD class and I was pretty sure most of the school attended it. At least most of the freshmen. Scuttling into the locker room, I changed in record time and hopped into the hall on one foot while I tied my shoe.

Stopping just for a second before I darted into the gym, I gathered my wits and pooled magic in my hand. I was sweaty, and my hair had totally lost its luster. I was pretty sure I'd already sweated off the light layer of foundation I'd applied after watching a human beauty queen online. I needed a glamour.

Projecting what I'd like to look like into my magic, I moved my hands over my face and hair, set a bright smile on my face, and tried to slip quietly into the gym.

Brooks turned and smiled at me. I wanted to join him, Jayse, and Francis, or better yet, go hang out with Estelle and Tyler, but just then Madison noticed me. "Over here," she called. "We're working on running and sending spells accurately," she whispered as Tyler stood beside the teacher.

Kristi snorted. "Apparently that weirdo is really good at it and going to help us learn." She flipped her hair, a bit more violently than normal. "As if there's anything that freak can teach me."

Tyler heard her. The polite smile faded from her face, and her gaze moved from Coach Cates to us.

Standing slightly behind the Sparkles, I mouthed to her. "I'm so sorry." Tears pooled in my eyes. I wanted to run over and hug her and tell her she wasn't a freak at all. She was a great friend.

Narrowing her eyes on Kristi, she gritted her teeth and turned back to the teacher. I wanted to speak up and defend her, but chastising Kristi wouldn't fall in with our plans. Not that I was entirely sure what our plan was at this point. All I knew about it was that I had to befriend the Sparkles. We really hadn't gotten further than that.

And I wasn't convinced that I was going to be able to go through with it. There was no doubt in my mind that Kristi was a bitch, but Sadie and Madison seemed like decent people—other than their choice of friend.

"I'm interested to learn whatever they have to teach," I said instead of defending the remarks about Tyler being weird. I mean, they weren't even completely wrong. Tyler *was* weird, but it was the good kind that made people interesting.

"That's because you don't know any of the stuff you need to," Kristi responded sharply over her shoulder.

I scowled behind her back. She was really starting

to let the claws show. At first, she'd seemed so nice, but it had soon faded away. Most of the time, anyway. Sometimes, she was still nice enough that I forgot she could be catty.

In short, having female friends was confusing, and I wasn't sure if I liked it or not. At the rate this was going, potentially not. Although, if I removed Kristi, the rest of them were fairly great.

"Alright, I want everyone to pool magic in their hands and create a ball of light," Tyler called out.

Witches around us all murmured but still followed her instructions. I smirked at that. They might think she was odd, but if there was one thing witches responded to best, it was power. That was something hard to ignore when it came to Tyler. The stuff radiated off her in droves.

Which just led to more questions I needed answers for. Maybe the odd smell was something similar to with Sadie and Madison and was just an affinity coming through that I didn't recognize. But I didn't think so.

She was an enigma and I was starting to regret the decision to let her tell me in her own time.

My ball of light glimmered in my hand, but I toned it down, not wanting to blind anyone else. Around me, everyone else had their own little ball, some of them so bright, I had to look away. Some of them were so dim, I was surprised they even made one at all. They must have affinities for something different, otherwise, they'd never have gotten into Magic and Metaphysics Academy. The standards for gaining entry here were ridiculously high. They wanted the best of the best. And they got it.

"Pair up with someone who has a similar strength ball to yours," Tyler called out.

I looked around the room again, trying to work out whose was as strong or mine, or even stronger. I was holding back some of my magic, and it wouldn't be a good plan to pair with someone weaker.

"I guess that means you're with me." Sadie bounced to my side. "That's a nice change. Normally Madison and Kristi pair up and I have to work with someone I don't know very well." There was a sadness in her voice that makes me want to reach out and put an arm around her.

Instead, I studied her ball of magic, pleased to find that we probably were a good match for it. The soft blue light held steady and strong just like mine did, though I was hiding the natural green tint of my magic. No one seemed to think very highly of nature magic, and I intended to keep my true affinity for it as quiet as possible. Even if I didn't want to.

Thinking about it started an itch under my skin. I'd gone too long without going outside and spending some alone time with nature. I should make sure to schedule more of it in. I couldn't let myself get sick just because my affinity wasn't seen as cool. It wasn't like I had a choice in what it was. I was born this way, just like the others were.

"Exercise number five!" Tyler shouted out.

I stared at her, not at all sure what to do. I wasn't even sure that I dared to ask Sadie. I didn't want to seem as incompetent as I felt right now.

"I'll show you," the other witch whispered.

"Thank you." Relief flooded through me. My assumption about her being a decent person was right after all, it was good to be reminded of that.

"We need to stand about three feet apart, then we throw our the balls back and forth, making sure we catch it with our magic."

I nodded. That seemed simple enough, even if it was the first time I tried it. In some ways, my magical knowledge was a lot more advanced than most people in our year, but in this aspect, I was behind. I'd have to ask Dad why he'd never bothered with teaching me defensive magic. It was odd that he'd sent me out into the world without ways for me to defend myself in a tricky situation.

"Got it," I said a little belatedly.

Sadie was already getting herself into position

and passing her ball of magic back and forth to warm up.

That wasn't a bad idea, and I started doing it myself. It took a moment for the ball to detach itself from my hand and start moving, but once I got the hang of it, it seemed to work as well as it did for the others.

"Now throw it into the middle," Sadie instructed.

I did as she said, just as her magic ball sailed towards me. The two balls met in the middle, giving a soft flash of light and fusing together. Light danced along the surface of it, swirling blue and green together until it turned into a beautiful turquoise color.

Dread filled me. What if Sadie worked out what I was from the color of our ball?

She took a couple of steps forward and plucked it from the air. "I'm going to throw it at you now. The idea is that you use your own magic to catch it and throw it back. If you touch it with your hands, the other person gains a point. The winner is the one with the most at the end of it."

I nodded. "Got it."

The ball came flying at me, and I tried not to panic. It wasn't going to hit me in the face. I threw my magic out, only remembering to mask the green in it at the last second. The ball bounced against it and headed back to Sadie. It was like magical tennis.

"Whoa, a little softer," she called.

"Should we move further apart?" I asked, not sure whether or not I could properly achieve softer. I really wasn't experienced at this kind of magic.

She shook her head. "Control is part of the exercise. I'll just be ready next time."

"Sorry," I muttered, scuffing my foot on the floor.

"It's fine. We're both powerful, I've experienced what you're going through before. It took me a few tries to actually get it too."

"Thanks. That's really reassuring." And I wasn't lying. It was good to know I wasn't alone feeling the way I did. It didn't escape my notice that she was being so helpful when Kristi was in the room, even if she wasn't quite in the vicinity to listen in on what we were saying.

Sadie threw the ball back, and this time I caught it in my magic and defused some of the power before sending it back to her.

"Better." A large smile crossed her face.

I understood that. This was kind of fun.

We threw it back and forth for the next five minutes, gradually increasing the power in the ball until it could probably break through one of the walls around us. It was safe to say that Sadie was powerful. It made me wonder why she let Kristi be in charge when she clearly had the raw potential. I wasn't in a place where I could ask her about that, but I was sure I could at some point.

Tyler stopped us just as we were getting into the flow of it and started us on another exercise. And another one. I had to admit that Sadie was pretty good at helping me figure out what I was supposed to be doing, though I could tell this was only the simple stuff, especially as each exercise seemed to get harder and harder.

"Last one!" Tyler called, and everyone instantly stopped what they were doing.

Sadie dropped the magical net she'd been swinging at me. The idea being that I used my magic to help me jump and dodge her attacks. That one had been kind of fun, but I was glad it was over at the same time. I had some burns on my legs where her magic had hit me. It wasn't that she'd been trying to hurt me, but it was impossible to make some of the magic we'd been using without it risking some kind of damage.

Over by Kristi, Madison rubbed a welt on her elbow. Apparently, the head Sparkle hadn't been as careful as we had about keeping the damage level of our magic down.

"Build a ladder from magic and climb to the roof,"

she instructed. "Then do it again while your partner throws magic at you. You'll need to deflect the attacks."

I gulped nervously, not listening to the rest of Tyler's instructions. Heights and I weren't really friends. Add in magic being hurtled at me, and I could see this ending in tears.

"Want me to go first?" Sadie asked, clearly realizing how uncomfortable I was.

"Please." That would help a little bit. Or I hoped it would.

"Make a net for me?"

I nodded and produced one seconds later, making sure to infuse it with my will. I wanted to let her magic get through it, but not her body. It wasn't the easiest thing to do, but well within my skill set.

The magic glittered as she produced the desired ladder and scrambled to the top. Okay then, that didn't look too bad.

"Catch me with the net?" she shouted from the top.

"Got it!" I put all of my focus into keeping the net strong and she dropped down into it. She bounced like a gymnast and dismounted beautifully. If I fell from that height, I'd hit the net like a rock.

"Now try with the magic."

I focused, feeling more nervous about this one but

knowing I had no way out of it. Throwing magic at my friend seemed like a mean thing to do, even if she knew and accepted what the exercise was.

Sadie clambered up the ladder again, slower than before, but only because she was spending the time deflecting my fake attacks. I tried to keep them tame enough that they wouldn't hurt, at the same time as keeping the net strong enough to catch her if she fell.

"That was awesome!" she shouted from the top. "Net again?"

"Go ahead," I shouted back, strengthening the net as the ladder disappeared and she dropped down.

"Woohoo!" she cried on the way down. "I love doing that."

"Sadie," Kristi chided.

The joy seeped away from her face. "Sorry," she muttered.

"Switch. You go work with Madison." There was no question in her voice, which worried me.

I'd been sneaking glances at the other two Sparkles when I'd had the chance, and it had been very clear that neither of them had the same level of magical ability that Sadie and I had.

And now Kristi was spotting for me.

"Would you mind creating a net for me?" Nerves fluttered in my stomach as I asked. A little part of me was convinced that she was going to say no to me.

She didn't seem to care much about class. Though she must be intelligent, or she'd never have gotten in.

"Sure." She flicked her hand and a net appeared, with flimsy threads and parts that looked like it would snap the moment any weight was put on it.

But I didn't say anything. I had a feeling she'd split Sadie and me up for a reason, and I was just going to have to deal with it.

With a wave of my hand, I created a ladder in front of me. Now all I had to do was pluck up the courage to actually climb it. Not willing to trust Kristi's net, I created a rope from magic that attached to the top of the ladder and looped around my waist. It wouldn't do much if I did fall, but it was better than nothing, and right now I would have to take it.

I put my hands on the rungs and began to climb, imagining my ladder was a sturdy vine growing from the earth. That helped calm my nerves slightly, and I made my way to the top, where I certainly wouldn't be doing anything like letting Kristi catch me in her net. She'd probably let me fall straight through and to the floor.

I reached out with a shaking hand and touched the ceiling, feeling a sense of victory spread through me. I hadn't thought I was going to be able to do it, and yet, I had. Now I just had to go through with the rest of the exercise.

The climb down didn't seem too bad until I was near the bottom and my ladder began to shake. My eyes widened and my legs stiffened as the panic set in. What was going to happen if I fell? For some reason, the floor didn't seem to have much bounce in it. If I fell, it was going to hurt.

The ladder shook again, and I clung on. Something twinged through me, almost as if my magic itself was being attacked. I frowned. That made sense.

I looked down at Kristi, to find her firing darts of magic at my ladder. Clearly, she hadn't understood the instructions.

"Kristi," I called.

She ignored me. And more worryingly still, her net flashed and fizzled out of being.

Uh-oh.

My panic caused my hold on my magic to slip, and my ladder followed her net, leaving me hurtling towards the floor.

An unbidden scream rushed from my lips, and I closed my eyes, hoping that someone would think quick enough to throw up some magic and catch me with it.

But it wasn't magic that met my back. It wasn't the floor either. I landed hard, pushing the air out of my lungs, but not hard enough to really hurt me. Just make me need to suck in a few breaths. It actually felt like someone was holding me.

Slowly, I opened my eyes and looked up at a face I'd come to know surprisingly well.

"Francis?" I asked, blinking a couple of times to try and work out if my brain was playing tricks on me.

"Hey. You alright?" His concerned gaze met mine.

I did a quick assessment of my body before nodding. "I think so. Thank you for catching me."

"I'll always catch you, Boogerface," Francis whispered.

I giggled, despite the fact I'd just made a huge fool of myself, I actually felt pretty good. No doubt it was something to do with the hot vampire holding me in his arms.

He pushed me to my feet, and I went gladly, wanting the attention on me to go away already. I could tell the other students were whispering about my mishap. Being part of the Sparkles didn't seem to save me from clumsy moments of being laughed at.

Francis rested his hand on the small of my back, making it clear that he still cared how I felt after my fall. Warmth traveled through my entire body and fled the moment I noticed the scowl on Kristi's face.

Oh. Right. They were exes. Something I seemed to be conveniently forgetting all the time.

I stepped away from Francis, putting some much-needed space between us. Kristi wasn't someone I wanted to make an enemy of, especially when she'd take Sadie and Madison with her. While I was only becoming warier of the head Sparkle, the other two were growing on me, and I wanted to preserve the budding friendship I had with them.

"Thanks." I rubbed the back of my neck, the nerves getting the better of me. "Sometimes I doubt I'll ever get the hang of all this." A nervous laugh slipped out without me meaning it to. Now I just looked like even more of an idiot.

"We've all been there," Francis assured me. "But I know someone that can help. Brooks?"

The witch who hung out with Francis and Jayse stepped out from among the throng of onlookers. If only this class had a teacher who cared about what the students were doing, then they'd all be back doing what they were supposed to and not just staring at me.

"You wanted me?" Brooks raised an eyebrow as he looked at Francis.

"Remember Lou?"

"You've talked about no one else," he quipped. "It'd be hard to forget her."

My cheeks flamed in embarrassment and, without even thinking about it, I pooled magic in my hand

and pressed it to my face, using a glamour to cover up the redness. I didn't want Francis to realize how I felt when he was around. It would just make avoiding him a lot harder.

"She's not done PD before, do you mind giving her a hand?"

Brooks smiled, his eyes crinkling and revealing just how genuine his response was going to be. "Of course, it's my specialty. Are you free after class ends?" he asked me.

"Yes. It's my free period after." I'd have preferred another botany lesson, but maybe not with how I was reacting around Francis today.

"Excellent. We can make a start now, but if you want the full scope, we need the extra time."

"Thank you," I said breathily. Oh great. Here I went again. Attractive men were turning out to be my downfall. No wonder my parents didn't send me academy sooner. I'd never have received the grades I had if that was the case.

"No problem."

"Don't be too grateful yet," Francis warned me. "He'll do anything for a beautiful woman."

My blush deepened beneath my glamour. I hoped that wasn't true. I didn't want to be the kind of girl who fell for a bit of flirting.

Brooks gave an easy laugh. "That's my older

brother, and you know it," he teased. "I just like a chance to show off my muscles." He winked at me and flexed his biceps.

My mouth went dry. He definitely wasn't as jacked as Jayse was, but the definition in his muscles revealed that he spent a lot of time working on them.

Coach Cates coughed loudly.

"I better get back to the Vamp section," Francis said, rolling his eyes at the sound.

All of us knew that Cates wouldn't do anything about us not doing what we were supposed to be, but none of us were interested in slacking off. We were here to learn.

"Enjoy." Francis waved a hand at us.

"Oh, we will," Brooks threw back, before turning back to me. "Ready for some fun?"

"I-I don't think *fun* applies when it comes to me and this." I waved my hand around the room to everyone else playing around with their magic.

"That's because you haven't seen my method of teaching yet."

"Is that a promise?" I joked, slipping a little into flirtiness. Oops. That wasn't intentional.

I glanced in the direction Francis had gone, wanting to check that we hadn't annoyed him by doing that. I hoped not.

"Francis wouldn't have asked me to help if he

didn't want the two of us talking to each other. Trust me, we're fine."

"Oh, sorry." I scuffed my shoes and tried to hide my embarrassment. I couldn't believe he'd caught me feeling so insecure. I didn't want to be that girl. "So, what are we doing first?" I asked, hoping to move us on to the stuff he could help me with.

"That depends..."

He was cut off by the sound of the bell. At least we had the next period free and could focus on my magic issues.

"On?" I prodded once the sound had faded.

"I was watching you and Sadie. You just need to work on your focus and your confidence. The rest should come naturally," he assured me.

"I hope you're right," I muttered. "So, what do you want me to do?"

He went over to his backpack and pulled out an apple.

"Make it float in the air," he instructed.

I nodded and easily focused my magic. This was the kind of thing that was straight forward.

The apple spun in the air, and I had to resist the urge to make it fly around the room. That would just be a bit of showing off.

"I take it you're keeping quiet about the fact you're a nature witch?" he asked.

The apple dropped to the floor as my magic bottomed out when panic hit my gut. "What do you mean?"

My blood turned to ice in my veins. How did he know? I'd been so careful to keep it under wraps.

He held out his hand and a tiny sapling sprung up. "Nature recognizes nature," he responded softly.

I opened and closed my mouth, not sure what to say to that. "I..."

"Thought only the losers were nature witches?" he teased.

"That's what everyone keeps telling me."

"That's true. It's one of the reasons I don't tell anyone. Only Francis and Jayse know."

"And they don't care?" Something like hope flairs in my heart. I wanted acceptance like that.

"Of course not. What I am has no bearing on me as a person."

"Tell that to Kristi, she has bitch written all over her." Slapping my hand over my mouth, I hoped he wouldn't tell anyone I said such a mean thing about the school's queen.

He chuckled. "Now there's a truth. I never understood what Francis saw in her."

"Maybe she used some kind of love spell on him?" Though I wasn't sure if that was even a real thing. Probably not. But it turned out there were a lot of things I didn't know about magic. I hoped my time here would change that.

Brooks scoffed.

"What do you think of the Greenies?" I asked. I hadn't had a chance to actually tell Miss Green that I wanted to be a part of the team, yet all I heard about them was negative things.

"I've wanted to join since I started here, but I haven't worked up the courage yet," he admitted.

"Same. But I need the connection to nature and soon. I'm starting to feel a little off." But with class and the party tomorrow night, it felt like I didn't have enough time for that.

"How about we clear some time on Sunday to go into the woods and do what we need to do?" he asked. "I'm overdue some nature time too."

"I'd like that," I said honestly.

The rest of our session passed with ease, my whole body relaxed now we'd set some time aside for nature. I needed it more than I wanted to admit. Having some time coming up would do me good.

And even more so because it meant I could spend time with Brooks. Having another nature witch around was going to make this easier for me, that was for sure.

So long as I could survive until then.

CHAPTER 8

"Which one should I use?" I asked Francis shyly. I didn't want to cross Kristi, not totally, but I couldn't help myself around Francis. He was funny and nice, not to mention hot. I knew exactly which plant would most benefit the growth of English Marigolds. Humans were able to gain small benefits from plants in their holistic remedies, but we knew how to use the plants to provide complete healing, and English Marigold was an excellent pain reliever. If ginger was grown nearby, it intensified the healing properties.

"The aloe," he whispered.

Uh, wrong.

"Wait, no." He consulted his textbook. "The ginger."

There we go.

I selected a ginger growth bud and carefully positioned it near the English Marigold seed I'd just planted, feeding it with small amounts of my power. It would grow strong and healthy now, and provide pain relief to someone that needed it.

Sighing, I moved to the next plant in my seed tray, lovingly giving it magic and energy so it would have a healthy, happy life. Working with plants made me feel peaceful and happy.

"You sure you're not good at this stuff?" Francis asked as he watched me feed the plants with my magic. He couldn't see the actual magic, but as a vampire, he could probably feel a small bit as I manipulated it. Vampires were sensitive to magic, even though they couldn't command it.

"I'm okay," I said evasively. "It's not the worst."

"Uh, yeah it is," he muttered as he shoved a ginger bud into the soil haphazardly. Several minutes later, one of his Shift buddies distracted him and he walked across the room. Both of our seed trays looked the same now that they were covered in soil, so I quickly switched his for mine, pulling the seeds and buds out of his soil with my magic, then replanting them properly, giving them a boost of magic. He'd never know, and the plants would grow much better.

Smiling, I grabbed both of our seed trays and took

them to the front, writing our names on them with the marker on Miss. Green's desk.

"Wonderful job, Lou," she said. Lowering her voice to a whisper, she continued. "I saw you fix Francis's tray." Her eyes were on him. His vampire hearing was sensitive, but he seemed distracted by his friends.

When I turned back to my desk, I spotted Kristi. She wasn't in this class, but she stood just outside the door, at an angle that I wouldn't have seen her if I hadn't been at the front of the room, but she had a clear view of the entire room. Giving her a little finger wave, I couldn't stop the chill that ran down my spine. Why would she be standing there watching the class?

She didn't wave back, just turned and walked away. Creepy.

Francis was equally hopeless planting his next seed tray, which was a plant used to fight infection. This time I couldn't manage to fix it for him. We walked to the front together.

"Here you go," he said brightly to Miss Green. As he turned to go back to his seat, he winked at me, and my heart fluttered. I hadn't seen him flirt with anybody else, and I'd been paying attention, worried that his flirtations were just part of his personality and not a special attraction to me.

When he was gone, I handed my tray to Miss Green and looked at his longingly, aching to fix it.

"I'll do it," she said under her breath. "I fix all of them."

The grade came from how well planted the seeds were and if they were planted alongside their best companions, but that didn't mean she couldn't fix the ones that were terrible, like Francis's.

"Great," I whispered.

"You know," she switched to a normal voice. "You really should consider coming to the Greenies this afternoon. You're a natural. I can feel it on you."

With a quick glance around the room to make sure nobody had heard her, I tried to get out of it. As much as I would've loved it, I didn't want to commit social suicide. "I'll think about it," I said hastily and walked away.

I knew I'd think about it a lot. I really did want to go, but the whole school would be against me if I did. No sense in making my life more stressful.

"What class do you have next?" Francis asked.

"Magical history, after lunch," I replied, really not looking forward to it. My dad was obsessed with the history of all the magical creatures and he'd taught me loads. Probably almost as much as they had taught me about animals. If the teacher was a bore it would be torture to sit through the class. "See you tonight at the party?"

"Yes, see you there." His smile was open and genuine, and I really couldn't wait to see him.

Lucky for me, the teacher was great. "First things first. I know you hate it, but there will be various levels of knowledge here. I'll pair you up based on your knowledge levels. So, in order for me to know who goes where, you're gonna take a test." She handed out a single sheet of paper with twenty questions on it, ranging from shapeshifter history to the witch trials. There were a couple of questions about obscure paranormal creatures, and one about hybrid history. I knew the answer to all of them.

She collected the papers, graded them quickly, then called us up to her desk one at a time. She skipped my name in the alphabetical list. As I watched the rest of the students be called up, I realized Jayse was sitting in the back corner of the room. How in the world had I missed him? I'd been a little late getting to class because I'd run to my room to change shirts after lunch. Kristi had said something about not liking it.

Being late was starting to become a habit of mine. One that I didn't particularly like.

"Jayse and Lou." Ms Piper called us up last, and together. His hand brushed mine as we stopped in front of her desk. "You both aced the test. I want you to take this." Reaching into her desk, she pulled out a single sheet of paper and handed it to me. "Work together and be prepared to teach the course material in two weeks. Then you'll get another assignment."

We were going to teach her class for her? I wasn't going to complain, we had to do it together. Working with Jayse would be great.

"Thank you," I said.

"You may leave, and work on this any time you would like, but be prepared when you return." We nodded, grabbed our stuff, and walked out of class.

"Well, what should we do with this unexpected freedom?" Jayse asked with a wicked grin.

"Um." I tucked my hair behind my ear and looked down the hall. "Go figure out the project?"

"Yeah, we will, but first, come with me." He turned in the opposite direction of the library.

"Isn't the library the other way?" I asked as I hurried to catch up with him.

"Yeah, but I'm starving."

"We just had lunch," I said with a laugh.

"I didn't like what they made."

He led the way to his dorm. I hesitated at the door. "Well," he said. "Come on in."

Inching my way into the room, I was both terrified and overwhelmingly excited to be there.

"Who do you share with?" I asked as he walked across the room to a full-size refrigerator.

"Francis and Brooks," he called back. "We managed to trade roommates and end up together.

"How'd you get a fridge?" They'd pushed their beds really close together, and their wardrobes and desks, too. There was a small chest of drawers beside the refrigerator with a microwave on top.

"We hold the blood for the vamps on this floor." He rummaged around in the freezer and I spotted a blood bag. My own hunger reared its head, and I realized I hadn't had a drop of blood all week. I hadn't even noticed, everything had been so crazy. I should try to drink some while I was in relative privacy.

I knew his secret, maybe he could know mine. "Hey, Jayse, can I ask you something?"

"Of course." He pulled out a half-gallon of ice cream and a gallon of milk. After rummaging around in the drawers of the chest he produced chocolate syrup. "Want one?"

"Yeah, that sounds great, but there's something else..." I paused for a moment, wondering if I dared to tell him the truth. Being a hybrid wasn't easy, and the last thing I wanted was to reveal it to the wrong person.

Hundreds of years before, this one bitch hybrid

had tried to take too much power. She'd been the offspring of a politically powerful couple—one a witch and one a vampire. After she'd gone freaking nuts it had taken ages to subdue her, then the supernatural community went a little nuts themselves. The human witch trials were actually a hybrid purge, spurred by the pure-bloods of each species.

Nowadays, the death penalty for being a hybrid wasn't at all enforced, but people tended to look at us a little differently. It didn't help that it was incredibly rare for a hybrid to be produced from an inter-species union.

"Lou?" he prompted.

Oh, right, yes. Maybe it was better to actually speak rather than just think things.

"You know what it means to keep a potentially life-altering secret, right?" I said as I inched toward the fridge, suddenly ravenous and anxious to have some blood.

"I do," he said carefully as he pulled a small blender out of the bottom drawer.

"Here's the thing." I cleared my throat. The blood was on the other side of the closed fridge door. I could almost smell it. "I'm actually a hybrid."

"Vampire?" he asked casually.

"How'd you know?" Shifters couldn't usually differentiate vampires from witches by smell alone.

Some wolves could, but only if they had particularly powerful sniffers.

"Francis. He said you'd just claimed to be a witch, but he could smell the vamp in you. We figured you'd tell us in your own time, or not." He smiled at me as he scooped ice cream into the blender. "I'm glad you did, though. You need some blood?"

"I really do," I whispered, embarrassed. I'd only ever drank blood in front of my mom.

"Don't be shy. There's blood in the fridge, mugs in the drawer, and the microwave if you want it warm."

I did prefer it warm. I'd learned to feed on humans, of course, but I wasn't good at it. Mom had always entranced them for me or brought home some blood that I would pop in the microwave.

Without further ado, I did exactly as he said, warming the bag then snipping the corner off of it with scissors I found in the same drawer, as if they were there for that exact purpose. A stack of straws laid beside the scissors. I grabbed one, no desire to slurp the rich liquid and get it all over my face.

Turning away from Jayse as he switched on the blender, I sucked the blood down quickly, trying not to moan in relief as it hit my itching throat and aching stomach. It had an immediate effect, and my body warmed and animated. I hadn't noticed at all that I'd been growing sluggish. How had I missed the effects? Normally, I could last longer without having blood, but the increased magic use and stress must have drained me faster than usual.

I rinsed out the mug in the bathroom off their dorm room and dried it before returning it to the drawer. By the time I did that, Jayse had both of our milkshakes ready. "To wash down your lunches," he said, then clinked his plastic cup full of ice-creamy-goodness to mine. The milkshake was perfectly made, and we sat on his bed to drink it.

"Okay," I said and pulled out the paper. "Let's dig into this." We read over the paper as we drank, but it was hard to focus on ideas for bringing the project to life when Jayse kept touching me. My hand, my leg, my arm. It didn't seem to matter. All I knew was that I liked it.

We finally came up with an idea that I'd glamour us to look like witches from the time period we would teach as we taught the lesson, adding in humorous elements to keep it lively. We had a fair bit of research to do, but it would be great.

I couldn't wait to work with Jayse. He was so easy to be around. Especially now that I knew he would keep my secret.

"I should go," I said after we'd blown a couple of hours doing a whole lot of nothing. "I need to get ready for the party."

"See you there," he said.

For a moment, I thought he might lean in for a kiss, but at the last second, he straightened and stood.

"Bye," I called as I walked out the door.

Turning to go down the hall, I nearly ran straight into Kristi. "I've been looking for you."

"Well, here I am," I said with a smile. I'd had such a good afternoon not even she could ruin my mood.

"I saw you with Francis today." Her voice was carefully neutral. I couldn't tell at all how she felt about it.

"I figured you did." Looking at her out of the corner of my eye, I walked slowly toward my dorm. I really did need to get ready.

"You should know that we dated." She pursed her lips slightly.

"I know." Enough people had told me. This was probably the reason why.

"I wanted you to know that if you like him, you can go after him. I won't get in your way."

She stopped at the end of the hallway and looked at me.

"Thank you, but I'm not even sure if it'll be a problem." I went for a little honesty. "I really like Jayse, and Brooks was being so nice earlier. And they're all three freaking hot, right?" Maybe she'd become animated and we could just giggle about hot guys and move on.

"They are," she said without a smile. "If you're planning to lead all three of them on, you need to pick one and quit the games."

"I'm not—"

"Go get ready," she commanded. "See you at the party."

Wow. She was such a bitch. The more time I spent around her, the more I wanted to move forward with Estelle and Tyler's plans to... well, whatever they wanted to do to her. Revenge? Sabotage? Either way, Kristi had pushed me until I leaned hard toward jumping in all the way.

Seriously, what a bitch.

CHAPTER 9

I couldn't believe I'd managed to forget any of the dresses Sadie and Madison had picked out for me, and was far too embarrassed to ask them to bring one to my dorm room. With no other option, I decided to make do with my blue dress and use a glamour spell to change the color to deep red. I didn't want to have to maintain a glamour all night, so I did the best I could with my makeup and hair. The dress would be enough trouble. And I'd wait until right before I walked in to do it.

After spending nearly an hour perfecting my look, I said goodbye to my friends. They'd helped me get ready with good-natured teasing, but when I'd confessed how much I'd liked hanging out with Brooks the day before, they'd gotten serious.

"So, who do you like, then?" Estelle asked. As a

shifter, she couldn't use magic to fix her hair and clothing, so she'd let me use her curling iron. It was fatter than mine and would make nice big curls. I was going for beach waves since we were at the beach.

"That's not such an easy question," I said defensively as I used a normal electric curling iron and magical hairspray to make my hair curl just right. "Brooks and Jayse have been so nice to me."

"What about Francis?" Tyler asked. She was working on overlays for my nails. If they worked as she hoped they would, the magic would bond the paint she'd put on a tiny sticker onto my nail and stay until I gave it permission to go. It was a neat bit of spellwork.

"You know," I said as I finished the last curl. "You could really do something with these nail sheets, assuming they work."

"You're my first guinea pig," she said as she put the last bit of paint onto the stickers. "So, we'll see, won't we?"

After several hours, I was ready. All that was left was to do the glamour and I'd be perfect. My dress was gorgeous, the heels matched the red, not the blue, so that was good. My hair had come out excellent, and the makeup had gone on a lot easier this time.

And the nails had worked. She really had something there. I grabbed a small clutch purse Estelle was loaning me and headed out the door. "Are you sure I'm not too late?" I asked as I hesitated at the door. "It's nice to feel pretty, all dressed up like this, but I feel foolish."

"Stop it," Estelle said firmly. "You look hot. I mean, *hot*. Go flirt with your guys, and don't think I didn't notice you deflecting when you asked me about the nails."

I smiled sheepishly at her. Tyler gave me a finger wave. "Go. Have fun. Get some dirt on the Sparkles, but no reason you can't have fun, too."

"You two could come, you know." I felt guilty leaving them to go party, especially considering they'd helped me get ready.

"I'd rather rip out my nails, paint them, then put them back on," Tyler said dryly.

"I'd rather help her," Estelle said with her lip curled. "Go!"

I went. Shutting the door behind me, I walked down a floor, then all the way across the academy to the boys' side of the school, surprised at how well my feet were holding up in the heels. Kristi had said if you bought the right styles, they don't hurt. Maybe she'd been right.

I halfway figured some alarm to go off as I hesitated at the door to the guys' side. Knocking quickly before I lost my nerve, I nearly panicked when I remembered I hadn't done the glamour. Looking around the foyer to make sure nobody was there to see, I was impressed at the setup. A roaring fire warmed the room from the January chill, and couches and overstuffed seats were strewn about for easy socializing.

Filling my hands with extra magic, I ran them over the dress, imagining it turning into a deep ruby red. As I finished, I decided to put the image of my perfect makeup and hair over the top of the work I'd done. At least then if I got hot dancing or something, I'd look fresh from the salon chair like I did right at this moment. I managed to get my hands over my hair, but as I covered my face, the door jerked open.

"Booger face!" Francis said excitedly. "Come in, I hoped you'd come."

Pulling my hands away from my face, I saw Francis walking away. "Up here," he called, already halfway up the stairs. "We're having it in the tower, where they used to imprison maidens. I was pretty sure he turned to wink at me, but the lighting in the cold stone staircase was horrible. Small windows gave a bit of light every few feet, but it had been an overcast day, and not much light filtered through.

He opened the door for me and I stepped through

into a large circular room. It was the vision of what I'd pictured an imprisoned maiden's tower to look.

As I stepped into the light, everyone looked at me. I knew I was too late. I should have tried harder to make it on time. Now all the attention was on me. What if I tripped or something?

Magical light helped the candles keep the room bright enough to see clearly. Kristi and the Sparkles stood by a big door that was thrown open to the evening air, several students out on the balcony.

As one, the staring students began to laugh, sniggering behind their hands, or in the case of Zeke, the jerk that had hit on me my first day, actually pointing and openly guffawing.

"What's going on?" I whispered.

"I don't know," Francis said as he turned around and looked at me. "Oh, no."

"What?" I asked. He was staring at me like I'd lost my mind.

"Did you try to do a glamour right before you came in?" he asked in a whisper. I nodded my head as my fellow students laughed harder and harder. Zeke fell to the floor, clutching his side. "You've got boogers all over your face," he said. "Like, a lot."

Gasping, I touched my face. Little lumps were all over it. "No," I said with a sob, turning and running from the room. As I started down the steps, I removed the glamour, turning my dress blue and removing the disgusting boogers. I just looked like me again, pretty and ready to party.

What would I do now? How could I ever show my face here again?

Running down the stairs, I kept one hand on the stone wall because my eyes were too full of unshed tears to see where I stepped.

"Hey," someone called as I brushed past. "What's wrong?"

I heard footsteps behind me, rapidly following my progression. Throwing open the door at the foot of the stairs, I ran through as fast as I could in four-inch heels. A hand closed on my arm.

"Stop." The male voice was commanding, and though I didn't have to, I stopped and turned to look at him. To my surprise, it was Brooks.

"Leave me alone," I whispered. "Please."

"What the hell happened?" he asked.

Jayse slammed out the door behind us, nearly barreling right into us. "What happened?" he boomed.

"I have no idea." My voice wouldn't rise out of a

whisper. "It was a joke between Francis and me, and then it was happening. I don't know how."

Brooks's hand was still on my arm, and he used it to guide me to one of the couches. "Sit down and explain what happened."

"I can't." My heart was broken. Not only had my glamour gone wrong, but the entire school had been there to see it, and especially Francis. And Jayse. I wasn't sure which of them bothered me more. And to make matters worse, I just realized that I'd forgotten to call my parents. They were going to be so upset with me.

"She walked into the room with her face covered in something." Jayse sat on one side of me and Brooks the other. It was comforting to have one of them on either side of me. "I couldn't tell what it was, but the room was laughing pretty hard."

"It was boogers," I said in a whisper so soft they couldn't hear me, not even as close to me as they were. Oh sweet Demeter, could I say it? "It was boogers," I said firmly.

Jayse coughed, and I jerked my face toward him. Was he covering up a laugh? His face was deadly serious, but his cough had sounded awfully suspicious. He shrugged. "How did that happen?"

"I have no idea," I wailed, the tears finally falling. "I just wanted to make sure my hair didn't fall or my mascara run, if I started dancing or something. Oh, and I had to make my dress red. And then it all went so wrong."

Brooks grunted. "Strange. Glamours are generally pretty simple."

"I'd never done one before this week, and the ones I did were easy, I don't know what happened." A fresh wave of tears fell and I put my head in my hands. One of the guys patted me on the back. I was pretty sure it was Jayse because the touch was pretty heavy-handed. He had enormous hands and probably didn't know his own strength.

"It's not that bad," Jayse said. I looked at him through my fingers, trying to slow my sobs, but only succeeding in giving myself the hiccups.

"Here," Brooks said, conjuring a big white hankie. "You look like you need this."

Taking it from him thankfully, I covered my whole face and focused on calming down. "This is the worst," I whispered into the hankie.

"It's not the worst. Someone will do something embarrassing in PD tomorrow and the whole thing will blow over." Brooks put his hand on my knee and squeezed.

I peeked out from behind the handkerchief to look at him. "I highly doubt anyone will do anything this embarrassing."

"One time, I farted in PD," Jayse said. "Loudly."

Brooks nodded solemnly. "Very loudly."

"I thought nobody would ever talk to me again," he said, his eyes wide. "But they did."

I wiped my eyes and nose and smiled at him. "I'm sorry that happened to you."

"Me, too," Brooks said. "It smelled *so* bad."

A giggle escaped me despite the tears still threatening to fall.

"Since he doesn't want to confess himself, I can tell you that Brooks slept with his Mommy until he was eleven," Jayse said with a huge smile.

"Oh, come on, man, that's not the same at all." Brooks pulled his hand away to shove at Jayse behind my back, not that it did any good. "Lots of kids are scared of the dark."

"I don't think that's embarrassing," I told him.

"Fine, then he dropped his lunch on the first day of academy, and tried to magic it back up before it hit the ground, but his spell hit it wrong and sprayed food all over the cafeteria."

A snort slipped from my nose. "I'm sorry," I said. "I don't mean to laugh."

"Oh, go ahead," Brooks said with a wry grin. "It was pretty funny."

"Yeah, and Jayse was trying not to laugh at my

boogers, too," I said, shooting Jayse a teasingly angry look.

"I'm so sorry," he said. "I didn't laugh at first, but I was at the back of the room. I really didn't want to laugh cause that would hurt your feelings."

"It's okay," I said. "I guess it was pretty funny. If I don't take this good-naturedly, then it'll just get to me, won't it?"

"That's the spirit," Jayse said. "I don't think most of the kids in the room would laugh at you in cruelty, but they might've thought you'd done it as a prank. Once you ran from the room the laughter died down pretty fast. If they were just being cruel, it would've gotten louder."

"I'm sure some of them took pleasure in my embarrassment," I said wryly, twisting my lips in a sarcastic expression.

"Well, you always get some of those. That's life," Brooks said.

"Francis wasn't like that, luckily," I said. "He was kind. He looked totally horrified for me."

"What do you mean?" Jayse said. "Francis isn't here."

"Of course he is," I said. "He let me into the party."

Jayse looked confused. "He said he had to go home, some sort of family obligation."

"Maybe he changed his mind," I said with a

shrug. "Listen, you guys go back to the party. I'm going to go put on pajamas, and eat a bunch of ice cream."

"Are you sure?" Brooks squeezed my leg again. "Why don't we walk you to your dorm?"

"No," I said in a firm voice. "I insist you both go back to the party and enjoy yourselves."

"Okay." Jayse looked at me, then looked at Brooks, then leaned over and pressed a soft kiss on my cheek. "We think you're great, Lou. Don't forget that. If anyone bothers you Monday during any of your classes, you tell me. They'll regret it."

I touched the spot on my cheek where his lips had touched me and my heart fluttered. Brooks's hand tightened on my leg. "That goes double for me. Between me, Jayse, and Francis, nobody will dare mention it happening."

"Thanks, guys," I said. "Goodnight." I stood and walked away, turning back and giving them a dazed wave from the door, my hand still on my cheek. I was completely confused, all three of them seemed like they wanted to flirt with me, and I liked all three of them. Francis had been the sweetest thing in PD class, and now the kiss and the leg squeezing. Damn it.

What was I supposed to do now?

Working my way back to my dorm, I heard a

giggle ahead of me in an empty hallway full of classrooms. It was the only path I knew from one side of the academy to the other. Trying to mind my own business, I passed the open doorway that obviously had some canoodling students in it.

"Francis, we're going to get caught."

Hold the fuck up. Francis? And that voice definitely belonged to Kristi. Son of a bitch.

I tiptoed to the doorway, peeking in and hoping they didn't notice. Sure enough, Kristi had her bitch arms wrapped totally around Francis. They were framed in the light from the hallway and their profiles were clear.

Well, he flirted with me during class then kissed Kristi at night. If that's how it was, then I just had to decide between Brooks and Jayse.

Tiptoeing past the door, I hurried, breaking into a run as soon as I was far enough away that they wouldn't hear my footsteps.

When I reached my dorm, I threw the dorm open, panting and furious, angry and hurt tears running down my cheeks. "Okay, I'm ready. Tell me the big plan. Let's take this bitch out."

Estelle sat up in bed with a huge grin on her face.

"Hell, *yes*," Tyler exclaimed. "It's about time you figured it out."

Now we just had to come up with a real plan and take Kristi out.

Thank you for reading *Magical Mischief*, we hope you enjoyed the start of Lou's story! The Magic and Metaphysics Academy Trilogy continues in Magical Mistake: http://books2read.com/magicalmistake

ABOUT LAURA GREENWOOD

Laura is a USA Today Bestselling Author of paranormal, fantasy, urban fantasy, and contemporary romance. When she's not writing, she drinks a lot of tea, tries to resist French macarons, and works towards a diploma in Egyptology. She lives in the UK, where most of her books are set. Laura specialises in quick reads, whether you're looking for a swoonworthy romance for the bath, or an action-packed adventure for your latest journey, you'll find the perfect match amongst her books!

ABOUT LAINIE ANDERSON

Lainie lives in East Tennessee with her husband, three children, and an ever growing number of cats. She loves reading, watching TV, and procrastinating by browsing Facebook. L.A.'s passions include vampires, food, and listening to heavy metal music. She once won a Harry Potter trivia contest based on the books and lost one based on the movies. She has two bands on her bucket list that she still hasn't seen: AC/DC and Alice Cooper. Feel free to send tickets.

ALSO BY LAURA GREENWOOD

Signed Paperback & Merchandise:

You can find signed paperbacks, hardcovers, and merchandise based on my series (including stickers, magnets, face masks, and more!) via my website: https://www.authorlauragreenwood.co.uk/p/shop.html

Series List:

* denotes a completed series

The Obscure World

A paranormal & urban fantasy world where supernaturals live out in the open alongside humans. Each series can be read on its own, but there are cameos from past characters and mentions of previous events.

Ashryn Barker* - Grimalkin Academy: Kittens* - Grimalkin Academy: Catacombs* - City Of Blood* - Grimalkin Vampires* - Supernatural Retrieval Agency* - The Black Fan* - Sabre Woods Academy* - Scythe Grove Academy* - The Shifter Season - Cauldron Coffee Shop - Broomstick Bakery - Obscure Academy - Stonerest Academy - Obscure World: Holidays - Harker Academy

The Forgotten Gods World

A fantasy romance world based on Egyptian mythology. Each series can be read on its own, but there are cameos from past characters and mentions of previous events.

The Queen of Gods* - Forgotten Gods - Forgotten Gods: Origins*

The Egyptian Empire

A modern fantasy world set in an alternative timeline where the Egyptian Empire never fell.

The Apprentice Of Anubis

The Grimm World

A fantasy fairy tale romance world. Each series can be read on its own, but there are cameos from past characters and mentions of previous events.

Grimm Academy* - Fate Of The Crown* - Once Upon An Academy* - The Princess Competition

The Paranormal Council Universe

A paranormal romance & urban fantasy world where paranormals are hidden away from the human world, and are in search of their fated mates. Each series can be read on its own, but there are cameos from past characters and mentions of previous events.

The Paranormal Council Series* - The Fae Queens* - Paranormal Criminal Investigations* - MatchMater Paranormal Dating App* - The Necromancer Council* - Return Of The Fae*

Other Series

Beyond The Curse* - Untold Tales* - The Dragon Duels* - Rosewood Academy - ME* - Speed Dating With The Denizens Of The Underworld (shared world) - Seven Wardens* (co-written with Skye MacKinnon) - Tales Of Clan Robbins (co-written with L.A. Boruff) - Firehouse Witches* (co-written with Lacey Carter Andersen & L.A. Boruff) - Purple Oasis (co-written series with Arizona Tape) - Valentine Pride* (co-written with L.A. Boruff) - Magic and Metaphysics Academy* (co-written with L.A. Boruff)

Twin Souls Universe

A paranormal romance & urban fantasy world co-written with Arizona Tape. Each series can be read on its own, but there are cameos from past characters and mentions of previous events.

Twin Souls* - Dragon Soul* - The Renegade Dragons* - The Vampire Detective* - Amethyst's Wand Shop Mysteries - The Necromancer Morgue Mysteries

ALSO BY LAINIE ANDERSON

Demons and Demigods (Paranormal Romance)

COMPLETE SERIES

Series Boxed Set Coming Soon

The Devil's Delight

Chaotic Creations

Divine Deviations

Coven's End (Paranormal Reverse Harem)

COMPLETE SERIES

Series Boxed Set

Kane

Voss

Quin

Jillian

Academy's Rise (Paranormal Reverse Harem)

COMPLETE SERIES

Series Boxed Set

Hell Fire

Dark Water

Dead Air

Lucifer's War (Paranormal Romance)

COMPLETE SERIES

Devil's Consort

Devil's Assassin

Valentine Pride (Paranormal Reverse Harem)

COMPLETE SERIES

Series Boxed Set

Unicorn Mates

Unicorn Luck

http://www.books2read.com/Leola3

A Platypus and Her Mates

Magic & Metaphysics Academy (Paranormal Academy Reverse Harem)

COMPLETE SERIES

Series Boxed Set

Magical Mischief

Magical Mistake

Magical Misfit

Southern Soil (Sweet Contemporary Reverse Harem):

Literary Yours

Snow Cure

Printed by Libri Plureos GmbH in Hamburg,
Germany